Short & Sassy

A Selection of Short Stories

Sue-Ellen Pashley

Paperback ISBN: 978-0-6488018-4-9

Printed in Australia by Ingram Sparks
Cover design by Louisa West

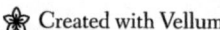

For my Family
With all my love.
Always.

Goddess Games

Sophie stood in the early morning light and sucked on the cut on the tip of her finger. Stupid knife. She wondered, not for the first time, if the Goddess would really mind if she just picked the herbs, rather than cutting them with the knife she was supposed to use. Her mentor had started to come to terms with it.

'You need to find your own Wiccan style,' she'd told her. 'Figure out what works for you and the energy around you and the Goddess will be happy.'

Sophie turned over her hand, looking at the small tattoo on her wrist that she'd got when her mother had died, four and a half years ago. The Jade Goddess—deity of compassion, family and love. She hadn't been going to get the Goddess when she'd wandered into the tattoo shop, still numb with the grief of her loss. She'd planned to get a tattoo of a cat, her mother's favourite animal, but the Goddess had...spoken to her, from a sketch on the wall, and Sophie figured maybe her mother was trying to tell her something. So, there she was, in all her small jade glory, a permanent part of her and a reminder of her mum. She brushed her fingers over the tattoo.

'You don't mind, do you?'

Getting no answer to the contrary, Sophie slipped the small knife into the pocket of her shorts and finished picking the plants she needed by hand—rue, yarrow, valerian, cohosh, rosemary and different types of bark, laying them carefully in her basket. She loved this time of the morning, with the bees buzzing around her and the world waking up to a new day full of possibilities.

Finished, she took her full basket inside, the cool air of the house a stark contrast to the already building heat outside, and ran her hand through her hair, trying to bring it to some order. Not that it ever worked. Her hair had a mind of its own, the curls springing up however they wanted no matter what she did.

The spell book was already open to the page she needed —old Merl next door had asked her for the tea to help with her arthritis, since it had worked so well last time. Sophie's finger followed the recipe down the page...and past it to the next spell. A love potion. She wondered if she'd ever be brave enough to make it. Not for Merl, obviously. At eighty-seven, she'd been married to George for sixty-three years and always said he was the love of her life.

No, she wondered if she'd ever be brave enough to make it for herself. It had been two years...two years and four months actually, since Kevin had left to 'find himself'. Whatever the hell that meant. He'd only made it as far as the next town though, so maybe he'd been easier to find than what he'd thought.

But a love potion... Sophie didn't want to find love that way. Someone compelled to want her—to want to be with her. No, she wasn't at that point. Not yet anyway.

The sound of the doorbell interrupted her thoughts and she frowned. Who could it be this early in the morning? The front door stuck, as it always did, and she yanked it open, flakes of paint coming away like sunny yellow snow.

Holy mother of Goddess, the sight before her. He was... beautiful. Brown hair flecked with gold that looked natural, not salon made, a chiselled jawline with just the right amount of stubble, and blue, blue eyes framed by dark lashes. She wondered if she'd actually completed the love spell in her sleep...

* * *

Christ, he barely remembered why he was there. Like a thief, the sight of her literally took his breath away. That brown tangle of curly hair with...was that rosemary in it? Brown eyes that reminded him of the toffee his grandmother used to make when he was a kid and even though she only came up to his shoulders, curves that made him forget who he was for a second.

She frowned at him. 'Can I help you?'

He had to consciously remember to swallow. 'Oh, yeah, hi. I'm Michael.'

It took a second for his brain to realise that this probably wasn't enough information. Jesus, talk about smooth. What was it about gorgeous women that made him unable to form complete sentences?

'I'm from...' he touched the name on his shirt.

'Michael's plumbing,' she finished for him, frowning.

He had an insane urge to reach out with this thumb and gently smooth the line between her eyebrows. Thankfully, his brain seemed to be working well enough that he resisted doing something that weird.

'We had a call about a plumbing emergency?'

She shook her head. 'You must have the wrong address. I didn't call anyone.'

'Are you sure?' He checked his phone. '6 Butterfield Road?'

She nodded. 'Yes, that's me, but—'

The sound of gushing water interrupted her words and he watched her eyes widen with surprise before she turned and started running. He raced after her, straight into the kitchen, where the tap had gone crazy, spraying water in every direction, soaking her as she tried to put her hands over it to stop the flow. Not that it was doing any good. In fact, it was probably making things worse. He came up beside her.

'Do you know where the mains are?'

She nodded.

'Can you go turn them off?'

She fled and he looked around, trying to find something to wrap around the end of the tap. A tea towel, a piece of cloth...anything!

Nothing.

He sighed and unbuttoned his shirt, wrapping it around the spout, trying to contain the damage. It was only a few minutes before he felt the pressure stop and she came back inside.

She was soaked and Jesus, everything in him clenched at the sight of her. God, what was wrong with him? He was twenty-seven, not seventeen!

* * *

Holy mother of Goddess, he'd taken his shirt off! She knew she was staring but she couldn't seem to stop herself.

Brown, well-shaped shoulders directed her attention down to arms that stopped just short of being too muscly. And abs...oh my...abs that rippled down to disappear into his shorts.

Holy crap, she was staring at his shorts!

Mortified, she managed to bring her gaze up to his face again. A face that was now a light tinge of red, which only made her want to touch him, just to see if his skin was warm. Dear Goddess, was it wrong to be wondering what a complete stranger tasted like? She thought it probably was.

'I'm so sorry,' she said. She didn't know if she was apologising for the tap or for herself. She suspected the latter. 'That was the weirdest thing. I wasn't having any problems with it before.'

He gave her a quizzical look, one that made his blue eyes crinkle at the sides.

'That *is* weird.'

She moved closer to him. 'What do you think the problem is?'

'I'm not sure.' He was breathing fast – well, faster than what she thought was normal – and she wondered what it'd be like to put her hand on his bare chest. If she'd be able to feel his heart thumping under her fingers...

She shook her head. That was just wrong. She needed to get a grip. He was a perfectly nice (very, very nice!) man here to do a job (that she hadn't known she'd needed), not to fulfil the needs of an obviously strung out, physically needy witch. Although it *had* been over two years...

Stop it! She told herself.

'Can I do anything to help?' There, that was better. Friendly, not needy. Or gropey.

His lips parted as if he was going to say something, but

5

then shut it again and closed his eyes for a second, taking a deep breath. She found she was staring again and looked away quickly when he opened them. She felt like a teenager, staring at her school crush!

'I'll get my toolbox. You might want to,' his hand flicked around the kitchen, 'mop up a bit of the water before it damages anything.'

'Mopping duty. Got you. Consider it done. Can do. Ten-four.' What the hell was wrong with her? For all things holy, shut up!

She grabbed paper towel from the cupboard and started to mop up the puddles that seemed to be everywhere, patting a damp strip against her face for a second in an effort to cool herself down. She hadn't been this hot and bothered for a long time. Probably for a long time before Kevin left if she was honest. Not that he hadn't been cute or that she hadn't fancied him, just that, well, things had got... boring by the end. Like neither of them could be bothered to try anymore. In some ways, it had been a relief when he'd said he was leaving.

The sound of a clearing throat brought her back to reality and she looked up at him from where she was kneeling on the floor. He looked even better from that angle. He was just standing there and she wondered if he felt the attraction as much as she did. Maybe that's why he was silent, watching her. Until she realised she was in front of the sink and he couldn't get past. Goddess, the humiliation!

* * *

He didn't know where to look, what to do. Christ, she was going to think he was some sort of psycho pervert rather than the professional he was. The professional who'd been building up his business for three years now, using the money his dad had left him in his will. Wanting to do him proud. And now, here he was, acting like a hormonal teenage boy around the girl of this dreams.

Girl of his dreams? Where did *that* come from?

He shook his head. Get a grip, man. She's going to be wondering what the crap is wrong with you.

Moving forward towards the sink, he put the tool box on the bench, trying to focus on what he needed to do rather than her movements as she continued to mop up. It was hard. Really hard. And then, suddenly, she was next to him. Close enough that he could smell her. Earthy, sweet...delicious.

She was staring up at him, her lips, pink and soft, parted as her eyes went to his hip. To the tattoo he'd got there three years ago, when his dad had died.

'The Jade Goddess.' She whispered the words and he forgot to breathe for a moment as she touched her finger to the lines inked into his body. His muscle quivered, as if rejoicing in the feel of her skin on his, and everything in him clenched.

'I wasn't going to get it,' he said at last, surprised he could actually get words out, 'but she... I don't know...'

'Spoke to you,' she finished for him and all he could do was nod.

She turned over her hand, showing him it's smaller twin on her wrist, and he took a step back. Bloody hell! What was going on here? The phone call, a visit that wasn't needed until he was actually here and now matching tattoos. With a woman he'd never met before!

'I don't understand. What does that mean?'

'The Goddess?'

'No. All of...this.'

'I don't know,' she said. 'Maybe it doesn't mean anything.'

And even though that didn't feel right, he was happy to go with it. Because the alternative was downright scary, no matter how sexy she was, or how much his fingers wanted to get caught up in her hair, or that he wanted to nuzzle into her neck, following the line of her collarbone with his lips...

Christ. Stop it!

He unwound his shirt from around the tap and despite the fact that it was soaking wet, putting it on at least gave him some sense of dignity. Soggy dignity, but dignity all the same.

'Okay, well, I'll have a look at the tap then, shall I?'

She nodded, biting her bottom lip in a way that made his blood heat to danger levels. Hot sun on the beach levels, where you all wanted to do was shed your clothes and leap into the water.

'Is there anything I can do?'

He tried a smile. 'No, all good.'

'I could dry your shirt for you.'

'No!' Christ, that was way too fast; too loud. 'I mean, it's okay.'

'Okay.'

* * *

She stood there, watching him, unsure what to do even though this was her house. To be perfectly honest, it was hard to look away and part of her was happy to stand there and watch him pull the tap apart. Really, really happy. Happier than was probably socially acceptable.

She leant against the bench. 'When did you get your Jade Goddess?'

His eyes flicked to her before looking back to what he was doing.

'Three years ago. After my dad died.' She heard a small catch in his voice. The same one she still got when she talked about her mum. 'What about you?'

She took a deep breath. 'Four years ago. After my mum died.'

His hands stopped moving for a moment so she knew he'd heard but he didn't look at her this time. She tried to ignore the small sliver of disappointment that lodged in her chest. She didn't even know his last name...how could she be disappointed?

'I'm sorry. I didn't even ask your name?' His voice was husky and even though he still wasn't looking at her, her heart increased its tempo, performing a solo tango on light feet.

'Sophie. Sophie Greenwood.'

He did turn to her then, giving her a smile that made her whole chest ache.

'Pleased to meet you, Sophie. I'm Michael *Black*wood.'

She laughed then, and he laughed with her.

'So, Sophie Greenwood, what do you think is going on here?'

She shook her head. 'I have absolutely no idea.'

He nodded and then put his tools away before turning back to her. 'There's nothing wrong with your tap.'

* * *

He watched her eyes widen in disbelief and the faint feeling of being set up slipped away.

'What do you mean? It was spraying water everywhere!'

'I know. But it's in perfect working order. Doesn't even need a new washer. The only thing that could possibly, at a stretch, have caused it, is a sudden change in water pressure.'

She cocked her head at him. 'So, what do you think? Should I turn the mains back on?'

It sounded almost like a dare and he nodded at her, trying not to let the nerves he was feeling show. God, she was gorgeous. And funny. And he wanted the tap to be fine when they turned it back on. He wanted this to mean something, even though that thought scared the hell out of him too.

She nodded and went back outside. He waited, trying to get his breathing under control and it seemed like forever before she was back there, at his side. She looked up at him and he could see the nervousness in her eyes as well. It made him feel better. Like they were in this together.

He flicked the lever of the tap and it came out in one even stream – perfectly well behaved. He couldn't stop the smile that came to his face or the balloon of happiness that seemed to be swelling in his chest.

She was smiling back at him. 'Well, will you look at that.'

And then, before he could change his mind; before his rational brain told him to stop and think about the fact that he'd only just met this woman and shouldn't do anything crazy; he moved closer to her. And, without hesitation, she turned her face up to his. Her lips were soft, softer than he thought they would be, and her hand came around the back of his neck, pulling him closer. He cradled her head, his fingers tangling in her hair like he'd been thinking about from the first time he'd seen her, while the other traced down her spine, pulling her closer to him. Her body moulded to his, fitting like she was always meant to be there. With him.

And all he could think was that he was home.

Project Cinderella

A ll my life, I'd devoured the stories about the girl being rescued by the handsome prince. Read them and believed them.

And so, I waited for him to come.

Waited.

And waited.

All through my mother dying and my father 'checking out' as a parent, no matter how much I loved and needed him.

All through him marrying the bitch from hell. I mean, they talk about step-mothers being wicked, but Valeria was definitely an over-achiever. And, of course, she bought two daughters with her two. Joy, oh joy.

Actually, it could've been nice; a ready-made family to belong to. Who wouldn't want that?

But Stella, who was my age, was a replica of her mother, both in looks and evil intent. Petra, a few years younger, wasn't all bad. She was just...complicit in the evil. Never overtly nasty but never calling them out on it either.

And I waited all though being treated like the resident slave. And I mean slave, not servant. There was no payment unless you counted the leftovers from the family meals and a small, closet-sized room off the kitchen.

No one can say I wasn't patient.

But there comes a point where a girl has to say 'enough is enough' and decide to rescue herself.

It took a while to come up with a plan. If I was going to get away, it was going to be for more than slaving away in a menial job in another location. I was determined to have a great life. One where *I* was in control of what happened to me.

And that's how I stumbled on to The Agency.

It was early morning and I'd gone to collect wood from the stockpile at the bottom of our property, determined to get my jobs done so I could read in the library before anyone else was up (the only time when it was possible). My dress had long since faded to a pale, insipid blue, with ingrained mud staining the hem no matter how much it was washed, and there was no maid to do my hair – I *was* the maid! – so it was up in a simple bun. I looked like the nobody they'd made me, rather than the daughter of a lord that I was. The birds were just waking as I dragged the small cart over the rough path and sucked in the early morning, crisp air.

As I came through the trees, I noticed an older man with spectacles and a grey beard leaning on the fence bordering our property and eyed him wearily. It wasn't unknown to have strangers come along the path, looking for work or directions but it paid to be careful anyway.

"Good morning, my dear, you're up early on such a fresh morning."

"Morning," I said, loading the wood onto the cart and turning slightly away from him. "Can I help you?"

"Perhaps." He ran his fingers over his beard. "But I think it might be a matter of me being able to help you, Isabella."

I froze for a second, the rough block of wood in my hand suddenly feeling very heavy, before turning back to face him.

"How do you know my name?" Anyone of consequence had long ago forgotten I even existed, let alone remembered my name.

He gave a small smile, gone as quickly as it'd come.

"I know a lot about you, Isabella Corra Bissette. Or should I say, Cinderella."

I flinched at the name. I couldn't help it. It was what Valeria called me when she struck me with her riding whip. Cinderella – covered in ashes from lying by the fire and unfit for polite society. I drew myself up tall, trying not to show how hard my heart was pounding.

"Who are you?"

"My name is Gerard Grey. And I'm in a position to offer you a job."

I narrowed my eyes and straightened the bodice of my gown. "While I may not look it at present, I *am* the legitimate daughter of a nobleman."

He smiled and shook his head. "My dear, I am in no way trying to impugn your good name or proposition you. I am merely offering you an opportunity for honest employment."

"What sort of employment?" I'd enquired in several places in town – at the seamstress (my needlework was impeccable; it had to be when mending clothes bought the whip for anything other than perfection), and at the

14

bookkeepers, the florist and the bank. The last one, I knew, was virtually impossible. The bank would never think of employing a female, so I'd dressed as a male. Stupid, perhaps, but it was worth the slight risk of getting found out.

"I am part of an organisation called The Agency. And I believe, my dear, that we could use your particular skills."

My heart continued to thud in my chest, but for a different reason now. I'd heard of The Agency. Only whispers, of course. Few people thought they actually existed, instead preferring to believe they were merely a story told to children to keep them out of mischief.

And yet... and yet, I'd overheard conversations between my father and other nobleman, on the odd occasion when he was actually at home rather than at court. These were the times when Valeria would allow me to dress in one of Stella's gowns and act like I was actually part of the family. I wasn't sure if father believed the lie but maybe it was easier for him to not think about it.

"Go one," I said, smiling at him and dropping the wood.

And that's how I began.

Only small jobs to begin with. Big enough to squirrel some money away but not enough to leave as quickly as I would've liked. Nevertheless, it was a start.

For once in my life, I was happy to be an unknown; a nobody. It allowed me to hear secrets, to find those who were doing the wrong thing, or hurting others. It was a damn good feeling, really.

My seamstress skills came in handy when I needed to dress as a man or as a scullery maid for another household, my bookkeeping skills allowed me to understand other's ledgers.

Valeria only missed me once, when I'd been stuck in a neighbouring town overnight, unable to get away. She'd whipped me for it—seven well struck blows around my shoulders—but I'd refused to cry out. Stella had told her to give me two more, spiteful cow, and I'd struggled to not strike out at her. Petra had, at least, had the grace to turn away.

I'd comforted myself with the fact that I had a wad of money my step-mother knew nothing about.

I'd been working with The Agency for six months, receiving my assignments on scraps of paper left in the woodpile and giving my findings in the same way. Every morning, I checked for notes, not sure who was leaving them, but grateful they continued to be there. So, it was a shock one morning to find Gerard standing once again at the fence, waiting for me.

I let go of the rope of the cart, hand over my mouth. Oh God, he was here to tell me they didn't need me anymore! My hopes of escaping crumbled to ash like wood on the fire and I wanted to run back up to the house before he had the chance to open his mouth and ruin my already pretty crappy life.

He must've seen the panic in my face, because he stood straight, palms facing towards me in an attempt to calm.

"Isabella, are you alright?"

I nodded and then shook my head. "Why are you here? Aren't you happy with my work?"

"No, no, on the contrary! We wish to give you a bigger assignment. One that should, hopefully, give you the opportunity to start the new life you wish for. If that *is* what you wish for?"

Tears were loitering on my eyelashes and I blinked to get rid of them before he decided I was an emotional fool!

Smoothing my hands down my dress, I took a deep breath. "Yes, that would be acceptable."

And now I sounded like a stuck-up idiot!

He had the good grace not to smile.

"There's to be a masked ball, one week hence, for Crown Prince Frederick. We are going to help him to escape Cassel."

I frowned. "Escape. But he's the Crown Prince. Of *Cassel*!" I added, just in case I hadn't made myself clear.

He inclined his head in my direction. "Looks can be deceiving, can they not?"

Fair point. He waited for my nod.

"Why does he have to escape?"

He narrowed his eyes. "How much do you know of the royal family?"

I shrugged. "Only what most people know. Cassel's ruled by Queen Marelle, who's been on the throne for thirty-odd years with Prince Consort Phillipe at her side for all of that time. And they have three children, Frederick, Giselle and Anton."

"Actually, they have two children."

I frowned, confused. "What?"

"Tell me what you know of Belvale."

I huffed. "Belvale? What have they got to do with anything?"

He arched his eyebrows at me, staying silent, and I sighed.

"Belvale Kingdom has two deepwater ports and, as such, are a rich country. Far richer than Cassel could ever hope to be. Their King and Queen have provided stable government for forty years but they don't have any children of their own to continue their line."

Gerard gave a small smile. "Very good. What you may not know, since it was before you were born, is that just over twenty years ago, the Belvale King and Queen *were* blessed with a son, Prince Alexander. The heir to the throne. Adored even more because they'd waited so long for him; the Queen was in her forties when he was born. However, when he was just three months old, he died, and they were heartbroken. They've never been able to have another child."

I felt a clutch in my stomach for them; these people I'd never met but who'd lived through such a sad tale. "That's terrible."

He nodded. "Indeed. However, we've since learnt that Prince Alexander did not die. He was instead, kidnapped."

Understanding blossomed in my brain. "Prince Frederick."

Gerard smiled at me like I was his favourite student. "Exactly. The plans were for Queen Marelle's court to say they'd found the kidnappers and, when they returned the child, earn favoured status and therefore, an increase in revenue."

"God, that's terrible! He was an innocent child!" I stopped, sucking in a breath. "But they didn't return him."

"No." Gerard's mouth thinned in distaste. "No, they kept him, raised him as their own child."

"Why, when they were perfectly capable, obviously, of having their own children?"

"Having only found out this information in the last few months, we can only surmise. It seems Prince Consort Phillipe determined it would be better to raise him and treat him as their child, so that when he was announced as the heir to Belvale, he would have an emotional attachment to this Kingdom. And hence, a much closer relationship between the Kingdoms might occur because the heirs have been raised as brothers."

"But how do they expect to get away with the kidnapping?"

"They will continue with their earlier story—that the child was rescued from kidnappers but it's only now that they've come across evidence to tell them who he really is."

"That's despicable. His poor parents!" I chewed on my bottom lip in thought. "But why not let this just play out? Wouldn't it be good if the kingdoms united?"

Gerard shook his head. "The King and Queen of Belvale are aware of the ruse. They were the ones who first uncovered the information, in fact. It's only through luck and timing that we've convinced them not to declare war, which would be devastating for both kingdoms."

I thought of the number of ordinary citizens, possibly slaughtered in a war because of this terrible deception of the royal family, dying for nothing. "Of course."

"We've negotiated that Prince Frederick will be rescued during the ball—he's heavily watched at other times — and taken home to Belvale. Once he's safe, Belvale will inform the Cassel royal family, who will need to pay restitution. Heavy restitution. They will also play out the story, giving a reason for Frederick—Alexander—to have changed kingdoms. Only in this way, can we protect the citizens of both states."

I shook my head. It was hard to wrap my head around such...wickedness. Although I shouldn't be surprised. I'd had to live with Valeria for years, after all. I had first-hand experience of wickedness.

"What do you need me to do?"

"You, my dear Isabella, are the perfect girl to rescue the prince."

. . .

And that's how I found myself in the front room of our house (the one saved for important guests), getting dressed by The Agency, like they were the proverbial fairy godmother. Valeria and the girls had left half an hour before in the only carriage we owned, after I'd spent the whole day getting them ready. Not a thank you between them—not even a backward glance as they left. It's as if it hadn't even occurred to them that I could go to the ball as well. And I was too proud to ask. Not when I knew I was going anyway.

I swirled a little in the dress they'd slipped over my head. It was the most beautiful thing I'd ever worn—blue silk that hugged my body in a cool caress with a low back and small crystals sewn onto the top of the bodice, and a skirt covered in a gossamer fabric that seemed to float like it was constantly stirred by a light breeze.

Anna, another agency employee, slapped my ankle.

"Stay still. I'm trying to fix your hem and you swishing about like a foolish chit isn't helping," she grumbled and I hid a smile. I'd worked with Anna on a few small jobs and she was the closest thing to a friend I'd ever had. I refused to dwell on how sad that made my life sound. Not when this was my opportunity to change everything.

Another woman, one I hadn't met before, tugged at my hair at the same time, twisting and pulling and brushing. It actually made me happy that I didn't need to suffer this every day.

Gerard was sitting on father's favourite couch, legs crossed, watching my transformation now I was decently dressed.

"You're to make contact with the prince once you're at the ball. He'll be expecting you."

"What name have you given him? Who am I supposed to be when I make contact?"

He picked up a box sitting beside him on the floor.

"We haven't given him a name. We felt it would be dangerous for you to give your real name and, given we don't have access to the full guest list, potentially problematic if we pick the name of a guest already going. Instead, you are to wear these. There will be no one else that will have anything like them and they are the signal to the prince that you are the lady to help him escape the palace."

Opening the lid of the box, he pulled out a pair of shoes.

My mouth fell open in shock. "Are they glass slippers?"

He nodded, and I laughed. It wasn't a joyous laugh—it was an are-you-kidding-me one.

"How do you expect me to wear those? I won't be able to walk in them, let alone stand for hours at a ball — or dance, for God's sake! They'll give me blisters before I'm even out of the front door!"

"They're lined and are as comfortable as any other slippers," he said, with a patient sigh. "The heel of the right slipper is also a key for the door in the west wall, where The Agency carriage will wait to take both of you away."

I sucked in a breath at his words, my heart seeming to stop for a moment. "Both of us?"

He nodded. "I've taken the liberty of setting up a new life for you in Belvale. It was part of the agreement with them. You'll have your own home and money to live as the lady you are and should have always been treated as."

Tears formed and I blinked hard, not wanting to have red eyes for the ball. "You did that for me?"

He stood, bringing over the slippers and placing them at my feet. When he rose again, he looked into my eyes, his face serious. "I was a friend of your mother's, many years ago. I'm only sorry it's taken me so long to protect someone I knew was dear to her."

Ignoring the painful tug to my still being styled hair when I moved, I leant forward and gave him a hug—there were no words to express how I felt.

"Yes, well," he said, patting me awkwardly. So awkwardly that I choked on a laugh. "We'll have a bag packed for you with new clothes, shoes and toiletry needs. Is there anything else you would have us pack for you?"

I thought hard for a moment. The clothes I owned were cast-offs, long past their use by date, and all my trinkets had either been broken or taken by Valeria for her daughters.

"Only a book and the money I've already earned," I said, moving to the bookcase in the corner of the room and pulling out a small book of verse and the money I'd hidden under a loose board in the bottom. "The book was my mother's. She used to read to me from it all the time before she died. I'd like to take that."

"Of course," he said, taking them from me and holding them to his chest. "I will personally make sure they're packed."

And then, with dress suitably hemmed and hair perfectly styled, I was stepping into the glass slippers which, as he'd promised, were comfortable, and walking out the door to the carriage.

Gerard offered his hand to help me in and I turned to look at him.

"Thank you," I said and he kissed my hand.

"The carriage will wait outside the wall at midnight and will only be able to remain for ten minutes at the most. You *must* be there with Prince Frederick then. We can't leave the carriage for longer or it will be noticed."

"Midnight. Right."

"Be safe," he said.

I nodded. I could do this. I had to. For our countries, for Frederick's real parents, for Frederick...and for me. I took one long look at the only place I'd ever called home and then sat back in my seat, ready for my future.

The ball was in full flight by the time the carriage pulled up to the castle and yet, still people flowed through the doors. It'd be easy to get lost in the crowd and perhaps difficult to get the attention of the prince. Gerard hadn't told me how I was supposed to do that, apart from flashing my shoes!

The footman helped me from the carriage, and I fastened my mask in front of my eyes. It was a butterfly, which seemed apt really, as a flurry of them were already swarming in my stomach. Actually, they were probably closer to bats than butterflies.

I ran my hands down the front of my dress and took a deep breath before making my way up the stairs.

The ballroom looked incredible. Chandeliers filled the space with a delicate, fairy-like light and swaths of ivy and flowers hung from the ceiling like an upside-down garden. Gold candelabras holding lit candles were scattered around the room, surrounded by even more flowers and ivy. I felt like I'd landed in a different world. A beautiful, romantic world where nothing bad ever happened.

I snorted at my whimsy. I wasn't here to enjoy myself; I had a job to do. Straightening my shoulders I moved further into the room, searching for the prince in the press of guests.

Thankfully, it was easier than I thought it would be. He was up on a stage at the end of the room with his family — well, his kidnapper family — and none of them had masquerade masks on. I stood at the edge of the room, watching him for a moment.

He didn't really look like anyone else in his family, which made sense. I mean, it wasn't as if they were all blond and he was the only dark-haired one there, but there were subtle differences. Unlike the man posing as his father, Prince Frederick was tall with wide shoulders, accentuated by the dark blue jacket he wore. I could see, objectively of course, why Petra and Stella mooned over him. His thick, dark hair and square jaw, dimpled with a cleft, certainly made him hard to ignore.

But that was beside the point. It wouldn't matter if he was short and bald, I had a job to do.

Party goers were making their way to the stage, bowing and curtsying to the royal family, hoping, I guessed, to be noticed. And it seemed to be the only way I was going to get close enough to Frederick to show him the glass slippers, so he'd know who I was.

I took my place in the line and waited my turn, ignoring the feeling of my organs trying to turn themselves inside out. This was so different from my other jobs, where I could sneak around and be part of the background. Unseen.

Here, I was on display.

Finally, it was my turn. I smiled, feeling at least a little hidden behind my mask, and lifted the hem of my dress high enough to show my slippers before I sank into a curtsey. Prince Frederick's eyes widened slightly — thank God. Because I didn't know what else I could do if he wasn't observant. The Queen, settled on her throne, smiled and nodded and then looked behind me. I'd been dismissed. Not that I really cared. I'd accomplished the first part of my mission, at least.

Glancing at Frederick as I turned to leave, he nodded, just the smallest amount and I let out a long, slow breath.

I moved around the ballroom for the next half hour, waiting for the receiving line to finish so Frederick would be free to mingle with guests. Valeria, dressed in scarlet with feathers on her mask like an overgrown bird, was standing with my step-sisters on one of the slightly elevated platforms at the edges of the room, as if hoping to catch the prince's eye, and I made sure I didn't go anywhere near them.

A few men asked me to dance, one who smelt strongly of onions, but I made my excuses and kept circulating. The waiting definitely wasn't doing anything for my nerves!

Finally—finally!—the reception line finished and I moved up closer to the stage. Frederick bowed to his parents, his eyes searching the crowd until they met mine. He made his way over to me, the crowd parting for him and, for some ridiculous reason, my heart thumped in my chest. Nerves—that's what it had to be...

His eyes were the first thing I noticed. They were a startling, clear green, like new spring growth, framed by dark lashes. Wow!

I was thankful I stopped myself saying that out loud but, honestly; it was a close call.

He bowed to me and I curtsied in return.

"Would you do me the honour of the next dance?" he said, smiling.

Holy crap, even his voice did weird things to my insides. It was all dark and smooth, like melted chocolate.

"Off course." I tried not to be freaked out by the amount of people watching us as we made our way to the dance floor, but it felt like my face was a flaming, red beacon.

He put his arm around me, his fingers splayed across my

back. I hadn't really understood how low my dress dipped until I felt his skin on mine...

"So, do you come here often?" he said.

I raised an eyebrow—totally lost on him with my mask but it made me feel better.

"Only when there's a prince in need of saving." I didn't bother to hide the sharp sarcasm in my voice. He might think this was all fun and games but if they caught me taking the prince from the palace, it wouldn't be a slap on the wrist. I'd be dragged away, probably never to be seen again.

"Sorry," he said, grimacing slightly. "Nerves make me say stupid things. So, what's the plan? I have to say, I wasn't expecting them to send someone quite so...well, quite so beautiful, really. And I don't mean that as a line!" He hurried the words out. "Pure observation. I thought they'd send someone less...noteworthy."

My stupid, pathetic, ash covered heart fluttered at the fact he thought I was beautiful. Fluttered! I pressed my lips together for a moment. God, get a grip! This was going to set me up in my new life. There was no time for fluttering or compliments.

"Just before midnight, a carriage will waiting outside the west wall gate."

He swung me around, having no trouble keeping time with the music despite our conversation, his arms solid in their hold on me. "It's locked and guarded. My parents—" He stopped and took a deep breath. "I mean, the Queen and Prince Consort have always kept the palace gates locked. They've told us it's for our own protection but now, I doubt that was the real reason."

I could hear the hurt and confusion in his own voice, the grief he carried, and my heart went out to him. It was something I'd lived with for many years—not fitting into my own life. I squeezed his hand in sympathy and his eyes met mine before he gave me a small smile.

"I have the key," I said, my voice low. "And The Agency will take care of the guards. But it must be at midnight. Not before. It'll be too noticeable if you leave now but by midnight, people will be in their cups enough that you may not be missed straight away. And from what we understand, they're going to make the announcement of your real identity at half past the midnight hour, so we won't be able to wait longer than that."

He nodded, and for a few minutes, we were quiet as he whirled me around the dance floor. He was a very good dancer but then, I'd have expected nothing less. I allowed myself to enjoy it for a few minutes, feeling like a proper lady.

"Can I know the name of my rescuer?"

I hesitated. But there was nothing wrong with him knowing my name, surely.

"Isabella."

"Isabella." God, my name on his lips made my insides go mushy. "Can I call you Issy?"

"Only if I can call you Freddie."

He grinned at me. "Fair enough. Isabella it is."

I smiled back at him, even though it felt like I shouldn't. This wasn't a social outing; I wasn't even a real guest at the ball. This was work! But he was just so damned likable. And hot. Really hot.

"Where shall we meet?" I asked, knowing he'd have a far greater understanding of the palace than I did.

He glanced around, as if to get his bearings. "At the side of the podium over there," he nodded towards the raised area where Valeria had been standing, "is a door that leads to the west wing. Second door on the right of the long hallway is a library. I'll meet you there."

"Fine. Quarter to midnight. That gives us time to get to the gate."

He nodded and stepped back slightly as the music ended, holding my hand for a moment longer to raise it to his lips.

"Isabella, it's been a pleasure. I'll see you soon."

I inclined my head and we moved apart. He, of course, was instantly surrounded by young women hoping to secure the next dance. I was merely glared at by the same young women.

Glancing at the large clock at the far end of the room, I held back a groan. It was only half past ten. This night was going to take forever! As good a time as ever, perhaps, to check out the library; make sure I knew where I was going.

I made my way across the room, skirting around groups of people chatting and drinking. Already there were a few swaying as they flung their arms around while they told their stories.

"Madam, you are sublime!"

I glanced at the man in front of me and tried to side step around him but he moved in my way again.

"I say, that's not particularly friendly. I know I'm not a prince, but you could at least say hello."

I glared at him. "Hello. Now please excuse me, I need to see someone."

He gripped my arm, his fingers pressing hard into my skin.

"You are gorgeous, you know. I don't think I've seen you before. I definitely would've noticed—that hair, almost golden. And that luscious skin—I could lick you all over! Come. Dance with me. I would like to be your...friend." He leered at me as he touched a strand of my hair, and I shivered in disgust and anger. It was a shame, really, that it'd attract too much attention if I punched him in the nose.

I grabbed his wrist instead, digging my fingers into his tendons. He grimaced, groaning as he fell to his knees.

"I tried," I said, keeping my voice light, "to convince you I wasn't interested. I tried to help you save face but you had to keep going. When a lady says no, she means no. Do you understand?"

He looked up at me, his face white, and nodded. When I let go of him, he fell to his hands and knees, sucking in air. What a drama queen! I looked around to see if anyone had noticed. Frederick, dancing with a new partner, gave me a grin and a mock salute and I winked at him. Winked! God, what had got into me?

As I turned, I noticed Valeria off to the right, watching me through the crowd. She was tapping her finger to her lips, as if she was trying to work out who I was. Or was coming up with a plan...

I looked away, merging into the crowd before she took it upon herself to come and talk to me. My heart pounded, my palms slippery with sweat as I could almost feel her whip against the bare flesh of my shoulders and back if she found out.

No more. She'd never get the chance to hurt me again.

I made it to the door, and turned once more to check I was unnoticed, before slipping quickly through. The hallway was lit by glowing lanterns and I ran lightly down it, stopping at the second door, just as Frederick had told me. I paused, listening at the door, and when I couldn't hear anyone inside, slowly opened it.

The fire place had been lit and the room smelt of old books and wood-smoke. It was comforting—a place I would've been happy to spend time in. Perhaps in my new home, I could have something like this. I went to the windows, opening one slightly. The room was on the ground level with the slope of the land and, thankfully, slipping out the window would be easy. What would be more difficult was the fact that the garden was lit up like it was daylight. There'd be no sneaking in the shadows.

I chewed my bottom lip, trying to work out what we could do and it was only when I'd come up with a plan that I allowed myself to leave the room, re-joining the ball.

I watched from the sidelines, enjoying, for the moment, the splendour of it all. It wasn't something I expected to experience again and the music was too wonderful not to enjoy.

My eyes narrowed as I saw Prince Frederick moving towards me. What was he thinking? To dance with me twice could cause far too much undue attention!

"May I have the next dance, Lady Isabella?" His smile was not quite as easy as it had been previously and I swallowed my rebuke, nodding my acceptance instead, nerves sparking under my skin at the thought of what he might tell me. It wasn't until we were on the dance floor that I spoke.

"Is something wrong?"

His eyes flicked to the Queen and Prince Consort, watching the ball from their thrones.

"My father—I mean, the Prince Consort; I'm going to have to get used to that—just told me I'm to become engaged. Tonight. Before they make the announcement of my birth, I'm assuming. I don't know why except that perhaps they want me to be linked to this kingdom even more before they get rid of me."

"Engaged!" My brain was in a flurry of confusion.

"But... I mean... I wasn't aware you were seeing someone. Does dancing twice with me tonight make it difficult for you?"

He looked at me, a crease between his eyebrows. "No, it's not difficult for *me*. I don't even know the woman, nor have I yet met her. But I didn't mean to compromise you in anyway. I just had to let you know. I'm so sorry that I didn't think about what would happen for you when I'd left."

"No, no, that's fine. It fits well with my plan to get you out, actually."

"It does? How?"

I looked up at him—God, he was tall. And he smelt good.

Stop! Focus!

"The garden in front of the wall is well lit. I thought we could act as a couple besotted with each other, going for a stroll. We just need to find you a mask."

He smiled at me; a smile that made everything in me clench tight.

"I'm a good actor but I don't know that I'm that good."

It took a second for his words to sink in and my mouth fell open at his rudeness. He laughed, his eyes lighting up, before he lent down, his mouth close to my ear, breath warm on my neck.

"I'm kidding. It would be my pleasure to be...besotted with you."

I wasn't successful at stopping the shiver his words caused and when he pulled back to look in my eyes, his pupils were dilated. Like he'd meant the words he'd said. I didn't know what to say and for a second, my mind was a complete blank.

Holy crap!

"Yes, well, that's good then." I cleared my throat. "Is your fiancé here tonight? Will she be a problem?"

He sighed. "I have no idea. As I said, I haven't actually met her. I was told the decision; the deal, is probably a better word, was made earlier in the evening and like a good prince, I'm expected to do what I'm told, for the good of the kingdom."

"You've never met her? But that's ridiculous!"

He gave a weary smile. "And yet, totally something the royal family would do."

"Do you know who she is?"

"I believe her name is Stella. Stella Augustine."

I almost stopped dancing at the sound of my step-sister's name, and stumbled as he pulled me along.

"Are you okay?" His brow creased with concern.

"Yes." My voice was faint. "Yes, I'm fine."

"Do you know her?"

I nodded and then shook my head. And then nodded again. "Let's just say you're going to have a lucky escape. When's the announcement being made?"

He glanced at the clock. "After midnight. I'm assuming before they tell everyone my background."

"We should go then."

"Now?" He seemed startled and then collected himself. "You're right, of course. Shall I meet you in the library?"

I nodded. "Will you be able to get away?"

"I'll have to, won't I?" His thumb rubbed against my palm. "I'll see you soon."

The library was still empty when I got there and I paced in front of the fire, waiting, waiting, waiting. Just as well the shoes *were* as comfortable as Gerard had promised. I listened for every noise, alert to the possibility of being found before Frederick made it here.

After what I was sure was only ten minutes, but felt like an hour, footsteps echoed in the hallway. I moved further into the shadows at the edge of the room, away from the reach of the light of the fire, just in case it wasn't him.

The door opened; I was fairly certain the dark outline was the prince's silhouette but as I moved forward, a voice called out to him and I sank back into the shadows again.

"Prince Frederick," a feminine voice said. A voice I knew well. Valeria! God, what was she doing here?

Frederick turned and bowed in what I assumed was her direction, pulling the door closed slightly.

"Madam."

I wondered if he'd been taught how to do that; to seem both polite and intimidating all at the same time?

"How fortuitous to find you here. How are you enjoying the celebrations?"

"They're most enjoyable. Now, if you'll excuse me." He gestured towards the room.

I could've told him Valeria wouldn't be put off that easily. Through the slight gap left by the door, I saw her put her hand on his arm and for a totally idiotic, insane moment, I wanted to storm out and push her away from him. My hands formed into fists, clutching at the material of my dress instead. It was a poor substitute but probably a better decision.

"I am Lady Bisette, Stella's mother," she said, her voice breathy in a way that made me roll my eyes. She was old enough to be his mother, for God's sake, and he was supposed to be marrying her daughter! "When you return to the ballroom, we would be honoured to greet you and perhaps have you dance with Stella before the pronouncement is made. She is a beautiful girl, both inside and out. Far more beautiful than the blue butterfly you danced with tonight. Twice."

Bitch! And she was definitely overstating Stella's charms. By a long way. It was just as well I was getting him away from her. Well, trying to. The clock on the mantlepiece read quarter to twelve. We'd be cutting it fine if we didn't leave soon.

"Yes, fine," he said, removing her hand. "Lady...?"

"Bisette," she said, her tone tinged with the annoyance of him not remembering her name. "Valeria Bisette."

"Thank you, Lady Bisette, I shall seek you out on my return. I look forward to meeting your daughter and to the pronouncement."

She giggled. Giggled! I almost snorted in disgust. But at last, she turned to leave, thank God. Frederick stood where he was for a moment waiting, I thought, to make sure she was truly gone. When he came in, I stepped out of the shadows.

"Sorry," he said as he saw me. "I was waylaid by a ghastly woman; the mother of my bride-to-be."

"My step-mother," I said, grinning as I watched his face pale.

"Oh, I'm...I'm so sorry." He stopped and took a breath. "I'm sure she's lovely and I would've been more than happy to meet *you* as one of her daughters, should the circumstances have been different."

I waved my hand, taking pity on him. "No, you're right. She *is* ghastly. And she doesn't consider me one of her daughters. In fact, she'd be horrified to know I was here."

He stepped closer, reaching down to take my hand and kissing the back of it. It had happened to me more in the last few hours than in the rest of my life. To be fair, he was particularly good at it and everything in me clenched at his touch, like it wanted to leap forward and grab him. I sucked in a breath and hoped he didn't hear the effect he was having on me.

"Then she's a fool for missing the brightest jewel in the crown," he said as he looked up through his ridiculously thick lashes. Was there anything about this man that wasn't good looking? A part of me really hoped his toes were slightly gnarled. And if I hadn't been a self-respecting spy, I might have melted into a puddle at his feet right then and there. But I was. I said it a couple of times in my head just to remind myself.

"Right," I said, taking my hand back. "Right. Okay."

I stopped and took a breath. This was just embarrassing now.

"Right." I had to stop saying that word! "So, we don't have much time. I was thinking if we exit through the window, hopefully no one will waylay us and we can wander the garden like we have all the time in the world."

"Wander the garden like a besotted couple, as you mentioned?" He grinned at me and I swallowed hard.

"Yes, like that."

He attached the plain, black mask he pulled from his jacket pocket before bowing and sweeping his hand towards the window. "After you."

I tried to act normal as I moved towards the window but I could feel his eyes on me. God, did he have to be so...there!

"Let me," he said, climbing over the sill and lowering himself to the ground. He even did that with grace! He held up his hands to me. "I'll help you. I'm sure that dress isn't easy to climb in."

He was right, of course, so I accepted his offer, even if the feel of his hands on my waist as he lowered me down made my chest tighten like my ribs were protecting my heart. I turned and he tucked my hand in the crook of his arm as we moved away from the window, looking for all the world like a couple taking a stroll. Not particularly the 'done' thing. After all, there were no other couples around and we didn't have a chaperone, but at least the area was well lit.

He sighed, glancing around before looking down at me. "This is a bit surreal. I can't believe it's actually happening."

I squeezed his hand. "This must've been difficult for you. Finding out about your real parents."

Pain flashed over his face for a second. "Yes. I was ready to confront the Queen and Prince Consort about it straight away—demand...well, I don't know what I was going to demand. But Gerard convinced me this was the wiser course of action."

We were half away across the lawn when a palace guard came around the corner of the building.

"Quick, kiss me," I said.

"What?"

"Kiss me." I was a bit insulted that I needed to say it twice, really. "He'll know it's you if he stops to talk to us."

At least he didn't ask again. He turned towards me instead, one hand going to my cheek while the other went around my back and pulled me closer. His lips were light on mine to start with; soft, gentle, and then, without thinking, I was leaning into the kiss, my hand going around to tangle in his hair and I opened my mouth to him. He deepened the kiss, his tongue tangling with mine in a way that made me want to fall down and climb him at the same time. I could feel every part of him pressed against me. And I actually gasped when he pulled away.

His eyes were dark behind the mask as he looked down

at me and, for a moment, we stood in silence, looking at each other. It was gratifying that he seemed as out of breath as I was.

"I think he's gone," he said finally.

"What?"

"The guard." His hand moved over my waist and I felt every moment of it, as if all the nerves in my body had moved to that one area. "I think he's gone."

"Oh. Right. Right." God, I was doing it again! I clenched my jaw. "Well, let's get moving then."

"Isabella," he said. "I apologise—"

"No. Don't." If he apologised, then it made it wrong. And while it might have been; we weren't married, we'd only just met, for God's sake, I didn't want it to be wrong. Because it was amazing. My first kiss. I didn't want him to spoil it, even if I was never going to see him again after tonight. "Come on, let's go."

I was almost dragging him along but at least he'd stopped apologising! It was only as we got closer to the gate that we heard the clock start to strike.

Midnight!

We ran the last hundred metres, the dress tangling in my legs. The guards, as promised, were nowhere to be seen. I didn't want to know what happened to them.

"My slipper's the key to the gate." I leant down, trying... and failing...to find my way through all the material. God, ball dresses were so impractical for an escape!

"Allow me," he said, bending to take the shoe off my foot. The feel of his touch on my ankle was enough to make me gasp again.

"Here." His voice was husky and I took the slipper without trusting my own voice to respond.

I hit the slipper against the wood of the gate, as Gerard

had instructed, and just as it was supposed to, the heel broke off, exposing a key hidden in the end.

Eight bells. I inserted the key in the lock.

Nine bells. I turned it, hearing the satisfying click.

Ten. The door swung open and the carriage was there, just as planned.

Eleven. "There he is." The yell came from behind us and we turned, seeing a platoon of guards rushing across the lawn.

Twelve. "Hurry," Gerard urged from the door of the carriage and we ran towards it, tumbling in as it started to move.

I flopped on the seat, dishevelled and with one shoe, but I'd done it. I'd saved the prince.

It went just as Gerard promised it would. We rode for two days and nights, stopping only briefly to eat and bath. And as beautiful as it was, it was wonderful to change out of my ball gown. I wasn't sure what had happened to the second glass slipper; lost somewhere in the haste and tiredness of the two days. And while there was a part of me who would've liked to have kept it as a souvenir of how I'd saved not only a prince but also myself, it was enough to be free.

We dropped the prince at the Belvale castle; the reunion with his real parents, a tearful moment that I watched from the carriage, not wanting to impose. I was happy for him, even if I was going to miss him. We'd supported each other in the mad dash of the last few days— talked and laughed and slept on each other's shoulder while Gerard sat up with the coachman, looking for anyone following us.

Frederick had turned to the carriage as we moved off, as

if he was going to say something, but it was too late then and I didn't move forward to wave as we left. Perhaps it was better to end it like that.

The estate they gave to me within the borders of Belvale was beautiful. It wasn't my home, and there was a part of me that still yearned for the better life I might've had; should've had in the place I'd been born, but I was happy to make it mine. The house was bigger than I needed or expected it to be, and there were servants to help maintain it, stocked stables, a flourishing vegetable garden and a thicket of trees that I loved to wander through. And enough money that I'd never have to worry again.

I was happy, still doing the odd job for The Agency and enjoying the thrill and independence it gave me, although there were times when I was lonely. And that's when my mind would think of Frederick — or Alexander, as he was now called — and wonder how he was going with his new family. There was a part of me that wondered if he ever thought of me...and of our kiss.

When the knock came at the door one morning, I was expecting Gerard with a new job. But it wasn't. It was Alexander, in all his dark-haired, green-eyed glory. I'd forgotten how devastating his grin could be; how much it grabbed at my heart.

"What are you doing here?" God, rude! I shook my head. Get a grip! "I mean, hello."

His grin widened and he bowed, before reaching into his jacket and pulling out the glass slipper I thought I'd lost.

"I've come," he said, holding it out to me, "to see if I could find the girl who fits this slipper. And to see if she'd take the job of rescuing me again."

I frowned. "Rescue you from what?"

"My heart's withering away and I think you're the only one who can save it."

I laughed, rolling my eyes, even though my heart was doing somersaults.

"Cheesy," I said with a grin.

And as he bent down to kiss me, I decided I was quite partial to a bit of cheesiness.

The Flight

'God. Oh God. It's so small!'

Beside me, Sam sighed and reached into her bag.

'You'll be fine,' she said, straightening again, having found what she was looking for straight away. Of course. Her handbag was meticulous, everything exactly where it was supposed to be. I shoved mine further under the seat with my foot. No need for comparisons. 'It's the same plane you flew here on and you obviously survived that.'

'Yes, but statistically, that probably makes it worse.'

'No,' she said, flicking her hair over her shoulder. 'It doesn't. That's not how it works. Anyway, I have something for you. Something to help. Give me your wrist.'

I held out my hand like the dutiful younger sister I was, and she fastened a bracelet around it. The round stones were cool against my skin and I touched them with my finger. They were deep brown with swirls and flecks of gold and amber.

'Pretty.'

She nodded. 'Tiger's eye. They're a protection stone,

especially when travelling. They're supposed to attract good luck as well. And help with organization.' Her eyes flicked down to my bag and I shoved it again.

'Do you think it'll help?' I twisted it around my wrist, stomach still knotting as I looked out the window to the plane again.

'Imogen Celeste Brown, you are not going to die on that plane. It's perfectly safe.'

I groaned. 'Don't say the D word. It makes it worse.'

She sighed again. Those sighs were really starting to bug me.

'Let's people watch then,' she said. 'It'll take your mind off it. Mmm, check out the guy over there in the suit.'

I wrinkled my nose at her choice. We had different taste in men. In fact, we had different taste in most things. And we looked nothing alike. Sam was tall with blond hair and an ample chest whereas I was dark, short and flat. Petite, Mum used to say, like that made it better. The guy she'd pointed out had blond hair, cut aggressively in an almost-crewcut, and was dressed in a sharp, grey suit. I could feel the alpha male pheromones from here.

'Definitely not my type.' My eyes searched the small airport. 'Over there. He's much better.'

He was tall with dark hair and a three-day growth that had just a hint of roughness. Blue shirt that highlighted a nice chest and arms. Yummy.

Sam snorted. 'It's a shame about the wife and kid.'

'Shut up. Don't wreck my fantasy. It's not like anything's going to happen. I can imagine.'

'That's your problem. You're always imagining, never doing.'

It was my turn to sigh. I could feel this heading to another lecture about the sad state of my love life. I watched the guy with his family instead, tuning out her voice. His arm was wrapped around the woman and they laughed as the little girl acted out something in front of them. She was dressed in a rainbow of colours; a pink, glittery cowboy hat finishing the ensemble. A kid with pizzazz. I liked her. And then the guy swooped her into a hug, lifting her up and tickling her. Their joy was infectious and I smiled, even though my chest hurt a little watching them. That right there. That's what I wanted.

'Flight 713 to Brisbane is now boarding at Gate three.'

I gripped Sam's hand. 'Oh God.'

She squeezed my hand back. 'You've got the tiger's eye, remember? You'll be fine.'

I nodded; mouth dry. Right. The tiger's eye. I just needed to focus on that. But the plane seemed even smaller out on the tarmac and panic built in my chest, spreading, like it was systematically taking over every cell in my body. I twisted the bracelet, feeling the coolness of the stones, trying to remember to breathe.

Stuffing my bag under the seat, I fastened my belt with shaky hands, focusing on my breathing. In and out. In and out. It was only just keeping the panic at bay and we weren't even off the ground yet...

I looked at the people filing down the aisle instead, trying to keep my mind from going down dark paths. The guy in blue was waiting patiently as a woman tried to shove an obviously too big bag into the overhead locker. She must've asked for help because he pushed it in for her and she smiled at him. A flash of jealousy speared through me. Stupid.

And then he was continuing down the aisle, closer, closer until he stopped next to me, putting his bag in the locker. He smiled as he sat down, blue eyes wrinkling at the corners. A dark blue I could easily lose myself in. And damn, he smelt good. A slight whiff of cologne, but something else as well. Earthy. Nice.

Nice with wife and child that he's just left at the airport. I definitely needed to remember that.

* * *

By some great twist of fate, I was sitting next to the woman I'd noticed in the airport. Honestly, she'd been hard to miss. Dark long hair, brown eyes that up this close, had flecks of gold. Tiny, but there was a strength in the way she moved. I think that's what made me keep looking over at her. Brave enough to get on a plane when it obviously freaked the hell out of her, if the nervous breathing as the staff went through the safety procedures was anything to go by.

I watched her out of the corner of my eye as we left the ground. She gave a soft moan and I wondered if she was actually going to throw up. And whether I should offer her the bag out of my seat pocket or if that'd make it worse. She was gripping the armrests so hard her fingers were turning white but then let go to twist the bracelet she was wearing instead. Round and round.

I gave her a sympathetic smile. 'Not a fan of flying?'

She grimaced. 'Not really. And the statistics and facts don't help.'

* * *

He laughed. Dear God, even his laugh was perfect, like it was on the same frequency as my ovaries.

'No, they usually don't. When your stress response

kicks in, it's hard to persuade it that you're okay when you're still on the plane.'

I nodded at him. 'Right! Most people don't understand that. Everyone keeps lecturing me about how safe flying is, blah, blah, blah. Like I'm stupid and I don't know that already.'

'Is the bracelet a good luck charm?'

I realised I was still twisting it like some sort of maniac.

'Sort of. My sister gave it to me at the airport. It's tiger's eye. Apparently, it protects you when you're travelling and brings good luck. And something else too. Organization maybe?'

He smiled. My heart did a quick step and it wasn't because of fear this time.

'Is organization something you need help with?'

I felt the heat on my cheeks and he laughed again.

'I'll take the blush as a yes.'

Laughing with him, I realised I hadn't thought about panicking for at least a minute. It was a miracle.

'I'm Chris.' He turned slightly in his seat, hand out, and I shook it. It engulfed mine and I wondered what it'd feel like on my body, running down the side of my waist, cupping my—

Stop it! Wife and child. Wife and child...

'Imogen,' I said, withdrawing my hand.

Christ, I hadn't been this nervous since high school. I pushed my hand through my hair, not knowing what to do with it. Wishing she hadn't let go. She wasn't wearing a ring, but that didn't mean she wasn't in a relationship. God, I really hoped she wasn't.

'And are you heading to Brisbane for business or pleasure?'

Please be business. Please be business...

She screwed up her nose in a way that made me want to kiss her. Right then and there.

'I'm heading home but going back to work, so I guess a bit of both. But home is Sydney, not Brisbane.'

My heart sat up and took notice, like a bear scenting something on the wind. I tried to act cool, though. Unaffected.

'I'm heading to Sydney too. My flight's not till this afternoon. 3.10, I think.'

She smiled, one that made it to her eyes. 'We'll be on the same flight.' And then the smile faltered and I wondered what she was thinking. It was frustrating that I didn't have a clue. 'What about you? Are you flying for business?'

'No. Going home too. My sister's a single mum and had to go in for an operation, so I've been looking after my niece while she recovers. It'll be nice to get back to my own place. And the quiet!'

The smile was back, bigger this time, and I wanted to take her in my arms and protect her and make sure she always smiled like that. Neanderthal man stuff. Which was... different. For me, anyway. And slightly unsettling.

'Was that them at the airport? The little girl in the pink hat you hugged?'

'That's her. Billie.' I narrowed my eyes at her, trying not to smile like an idiot. 'You noticed me then?'

The heat was back in her cheeks. 'No! I mean, I noticed you because I liked Billie's hat and...'

* * *

I stopped when I saw he was grinning and quirked one eyebrow at him.

'Don't let it go to your head.'

The plane jolted and dropped and then dropped some more. I grabbed at the armrest and realised I was clutching his hand instead. Which would have been embarrassing except I was too scared to care, the fear pulsing in me like a monster, making my stomach twist itself in knots.

'Oh, crap. Crap, crap, crap.'

He squeezed my hand and the pressure was good, helping me focus.

'Just listen to my voice, okay? Tell me about your sister. What's her name?

I tried to make my brain work but it was paralysed. It wasn't a hard question though. Surely I knew that...

'Sam. It's Sam.'

'Great. And did you have a nickname for her growing up?'

I tried to smile. It came out as more of a grimace. 'Sister Sam when we were little. And then probably bitch when we were teenagers.'

He laughed and I felt the panic trickle away slightly.

'And was that her at the airport?'

I nodded. 'It was the first anniversary of her divorce, so I wanted to be there for her.'

'What was her ex like?'

I frowned. 'Okay. I mean, nice enough. They just weren't really suited.'

'And what about you? Boyfriend or husband waiting for you in Sydney?'

I shook my head, clutching his hand again as more turbulence hit.

'Imogen?'

'No. No partner. Not for over a year.'

He smiled and my heart did the quick step again. My brain was a confused mess, caught somewhere between fear and attraction. It was... distracting. Maybe this is what I needed every time I flew. A cute guy to distract me.

'Well, that's good to know.' He squeezed my hand slightly, his thumb rubbing across the top of my fingers and the lower half of my body turned to molten lava. I licked my lips, trying to get some moisture in my suddenly dry mouth.

'Are you flirting with me to distract me?'

* * *

My grin got bigger. 'No, I'm flirting with you because you're beautiful. And the hand holding's a bonus. But is it working anyway?'

I couldn't believe I'd actually said that. She was looking at me though, like her brain was still too panicked to think.

'Is what working?'

'Am I distracting you?' My voice was rough—like my desire was on display. Christ! Her breath caught, but I didn't know what that meant.

'Yes.'

It was amazing that one word could almost undo me. And then the attendant asked if we wanted food, breaking the moment and Imogen took her hand from mine. For a second, I wondered if it was wrong to grab it back. Yep, definitely wrong.

I massaged my fingers instead, trying to get rid of the feeling of loss. I'd never felt like this before. Especially after only—I checked my watch—half an hour. Half an hour! Scary. Scary and exciting and fantastic and confusing. I didn't understand what the hell was going on here.

* * *

He moved his hand back to his lap and I watched him rub his fingers. Crap, he'd think I was looking at his crutch.

And now I actually was!

God, look away, Imogen! I turned to the window, trying to distract myself.

'So, what do you do for work?' His voice was casual, like he had it all together, unlike me. But when I looked back, he was still massaging his fingers.

Work. Good. Safe topic.

'I'm a graphic artist. How about you?'

'Psychologist.'

'Oh no. And you get stuck next to the only lunatic on the plane!'

He laughed. 'Fear of flying doesn't make you a lunatic. That's my professional diagnosis.' He took a deep breath. 'But you could pay me back for the consultation by having a drink with me while we're waiting for the next flight.'

Yes. The word was desperately trying to push its way out. But I had to think. Think about... I didn't know what I was supposed to think about.

'Okay. That would be nice.'

And he let out his breath. Interesting.

For the rest of the flight, we talked. Talked about everything and nothing. Laughing. Teasing. And it was easy. Easier than it'd ever been before, even with my anxiety keeping me company. I hoped he was feeling the same.

'Cabin crew, prepare for landing.'

Shit. Shit, shit, shit. Landing was the worst part. And I had another flight after this. Why didn't I drive?

Chris touched my wrist, moving the bracelet slightly.

My skin tingled, the nerve endings feeling like they had a direct line to my stomach.

'Tell me what the bracelet is for again?'

'Safe travel.'

'Right. And good luck?'

I nodded, eyes closed, trying not to listen to the whine of the engines as we started our descent. Trying not to listen to the wheels lock into place. Trying to ignore all of it.

I felt him take my hand again and gratitude washed over me. It helped. God knows why but his touch helped.

'And do you think it's brought you good luck so far?'

I opened my eyes. He was watching me, eyes serious, and the feeling in my stomach travelled lower.

* * *

'Yes.'

Damn, just looking at her now, lips slightly parted, I wanted to kiss her. And not a nice, polite kiss. A hot one, pulling her hard against me. Everything in me clenched tight and I wondered who I was for a moment. Where was the calm, controlled, rational Chris my sister was always accusing me of being?

The wheels touched down. A perfect landing. I hadn't even noticed. She let out a shaky laugh and I rubbed my thumb over the inside of her wrist, watching as she nervously licked her lips. Christ!

The plane stopped and I stood, keeping the space in front of me for her to get out. All I could think about was her, almost touching me, the heat of her, the feeling of protection that loomed up in me. Even though she didn't need it. Even though I'd never felt like this before. Except now. With her.

She smiled at me as we walked through the airport and I felt like I was floating. And then we paid for drinks and settled into a booth, the lighting dim. My heart was beating against my ribs like it was trying to send her a Morse code message.

I played with the condensation on my glass, trying to sort out what was going on in my head and how I could say the words without coming across like a total weirdo. She was watching me. And I could see her own nervousness.

'You know, if you want to have a drink and then go, that's okay.'

She looked worried I might say yes, but maybe that was wishful thinking. I took a deep breath, hoping I wasn't making an idiot of myself.

'The crazy thing is, I don't want this to finish. I like you. And I've never felt like this before. Does that make you want to run?'

Her beautiful brown eyes were calm as she looked at me. 'No, actually. It doesn't.'

'Really?'

'Really.'

* * *

He smiled and brought my hand up to kiss my fingers. It was the sexiest thing that had happened to me in a long time and every organ in my body reacted. Then he leant closer, hesitating, a breath away from me. I reached up, lacing my hand through the hair at the nape of his neck like I'd imagined doing the whole flight and pulled him to me. His lips were gentle and his tongue flicked my lip, tasting me, until I felt like I was going to explode. I pulled him closer still, wanting more, and he moaned. Holy crap. I needed to stop. We were in public. I sat back and he looked at me, eyes wide.

'Wow.' He reached out to touch my lip with his thumb and I gently bit it. Bit it! I'd never done that on a first date. If that's what this even was.

'You know, I think I might need some professional support on the next flight.' My voice was embarrassingly husky.

He smiled, a lazy one that spoke of wanting and lust.

'I'm happy to help.'

And all I could think was that tiger's eyes were definitely bringers of good luck.

Change

Chapter One

He's waiting for me at the end of the pier. That's what his note said anyway.

I just don't know what form he'll take.

Whether he'll look like the Joshua I've fallen in love with over the last eighteen months—the funny, kooky, book-loving Joshua who's obsessed with G.O.T—or the Joshua I'd seen accidentally two nights ago, at his house.

The one who looked nothing like Josh.

The one who barely looked human...

God, why am I here? Do I really want to do this? Maybe I should walk away—forget him. Forget what I'd seen. Forget the anguish in his voice when he yelled out to me as I ran. I know I should be scared—any sane person would be. But I'm not. I'm confused. Confused and shocked and numb.

When I see him move in the fading light, watching me as I stand on the grass, I'm still trying to decide if I want to step onto the faded wood of the jetty.

But he looks like my Josh.

That's what gets me moving.

He looks like the boy who gave me my first kiss. The one who makes me feel safe when he hugs me, who makes me laugh when my shitty life gets too much. My shoes clatter on the wood, each step feeling like an exclamation mark to my decision. Closer. Closer. Until I'm close enough to see the small smile on his face.

And the worry in his eyes.

'Serena.' He sounds nervous. It's nice to know I'm not the only one.

'Hi.'

His hand reaches for mine and then, like he remembers why we're here, he pulls it back again. I'm not sure if I'm relieved or disappointed.

'Thanks for coming.'

I nod and then chew the side of my lip, watching him. 'I wanted... I mean... I couldn't...' I stop, taking a breath. 'What happened the other night? With you?'

He runs his hands through his dark brown hair, making it stand up. Messy in a gorgeous way. My hands itch to smooth it back down like I've done a thousand times before. But I can't. Not yet.

'Jesus, Ser, I don't even know where to start—what to tell you.'

I wait, expecting more words. An explanation. But he only groans, deep in his throat, and anger flairs up in me—anger driven by hurt. He asked me here to explain. That's what the note said. Explain why he's been keeping secrets, explain what happened two nights ago... explain how he'd smashed up the door to his room like it was cardboard when he saw me leaving...

'You know what, Josh, whatever. You asked me to come here, but if you don't want to talk, I'm out. I don't need this.'

He grabs my arm before I can take two steps, halting me, his breathing fast as he steps in front of me.

'Please, don't go. I want to explain.'

I arch my eyebrows. 'So, explain. What was that? What happened to you?'

He moves his hold on my arm down, taking my hand. And I let him.

'Can we sit?'

I hesitate and then nod, letting him lead me over to the seats on the side of the jetty.

'Okay.' He takes a deep breath. 'Okay. You know Joyce and Ray aren't my real parents?'

I nod. It was one of the first things he'd told me when we'd become friends, right after Joyce had thrown one of the crazy tantrums she was prone to and tossed his bag and guitar out of the still moving car one morning at school.

'Well, I got a visit a few weeks ago from someone who knew about my life before they adopted me. Or said they knew about it anyway.'

I gasp and clutch at his hand before I realise what I'm doing. 'That's awesome! Were they able to tell you something about your real parents?'

'Sort of.' He holds his bottom lip captive in his teeth for a moment. 'He told me he knew what was happening to me and that he had information about my birth and the years before I was adopted.'

'So, what did he say it was? What's happening to you?'

He shakes his head. 'I don't know yet. I just know I feel ... different. My body feels different. Like it's not really mine.'

I frown, trying to work out what those words mean. 'What—like you're possessed or something?'

'No. Jesus! Why would you go there?'

I laugh. It's not a happy one. 'God, I don't know? Maybe because I saw you change into something that didn't look like you. You were blue, for God's sake! And angry. You wrecked your room!'

'I know, I know!' He gets up and paces the wooden floor. 'This guy, Peter, he told me he has the answers I'm looking for. He said he'd tell me everything. I'm going to meet him tonight.'

'So why am I here, then? If you don't know anything yet, why did you want to meet?'

He squats in front of me, looking up at me with his dark blue eyes. 'I know it's a lot to ask, but I want you to come with me. I want you to hear what they say. So there's no secrets between us. I need you there. Please?'

I watch him for a moment, my eyes tracing the lines of his face, the tension I can see in his jaw, his eyes... eyes I know so well, despite whatever the hell is going on for him. So, I nod. Because what else would I do?

Chapter Two

The house we approach looks like any other house on this suburban street. It certainly doesn't look scary or weird and yet, my heart's pounding in my chest and my breathing's short and sharp. It probably isn't helping that Josh is looking like he's about to run at any moment. God, I can't imagine how this must feel for him.

I'm not angry anymore. Actually, I don't know that I really *was* angry. More hurt. Hurt that he was keeping a secret from me. A huge secret. But I guess it's hard to talk about something when you can't understand what's going on yourself. And the shock has worn off. It doesn't mean I'm not still freaked out, just... well, I'm happy to be freaked out *with* him. Rather than *at* him.

I squeeze his hand. 'Come on. Let's get this over and done with.'

'Yeah.' But he doesn't move. He's still staring at the house in front of us, its address written in neat writing on a piece of paper clutched in his hand.

I look at him, eyebrows raised, asking the silent question.

'Just...' he crushes the paper as his hand clenches into a fist. 'I don't want you to hate me or anything. Whatever we find out in there, don't hate me, okay?'

'Okay.' My voice is soft, gentle.

'Promise?'

'Promise.'

He nods like we've made a deal. Not that we really need to. The last two days have been crappy and horrible and heartbreaking. And now, I'm kind of disappointed I reacted the way I did. I know it was shock. It's not every day you see the guy you love change in front of you into something...someone... you don't recognise. Rationally, I know that. But what sort of girlfriend am I—what sort of friend—that I just left, not giving him the opportunity or time to explain?

He walks down the path then, and I walk with him, only standing back a little when he reaches out to knock on the door. It's answered by a man with dark hair, sprinkled at the sides with silver. His stern face relaxes slightly when he sees Josh, but he frowns when he notices me.

'Joshua, glad you could come. Who's your friend?'

Josh stands taller, reaching behind to take my hand. 'This is Serena. My girlfriend. She's already seen me... change... or whatever the hell I did. I'm not coming in without her.'

The silence is heavy as the man's frown deepens. He looks like he wants to object—wants to tell me to go—but finally, he sighs.

'Fine.' His eyes meet mine, his gaze intense. 'We expect absolute secrecy. No exceptions. And there'll be consequences if this isn't kept.'

The threat is obvious. Clear enough that I don't need to ask what the consequences might be. I want to push against him; against the threat, because how dare he! But I'm here for Josh, and who am I going to tell anyway? So, I nod.

He moves aside, ushering us in and closing the door, before leading us down a hallway, past closed doors, to the back of the house. There are two other people there—another man and a woman. Josh stops at the door, looking at Peter, the hesitation clear on his face.

'I assumed it was just going to be us.'

Peter looks at the others and then back.

'I thought it was important that you have others you can ask questions of, too. And so you know there's more of us.'

'More?' Josh looks like he's about to throw up and I want to grab his hand and run. Run, run, run. Tell him it doesn't matter. That I don't care. But then the woman's standing and moving towards us, her eyes gentle.

'Welcome. I'm Avril.'

She holds out her hand and Josh takes it.

'I'm Joshua. Josh.'

She nods and then looks at me. I'm so focused on Josh, it takes me a second to realise what she wants.

'Oh. I'm Serena.'

She smiles. 'Come and join us.'

And then Josh is moving into the room and I'm following him, sitting on a dark brown couch, flanked by the chairs of the two men.

'This is Tom,' Peter says, gesturing to the other man, who nods in greeting.

There's silence—an impatient silence, waiting to be filled—but it's as if no one wants to start.

Peter clears his throat. 'So, Joshua, what do you know of your childhood?'

Josh frowns. 'Not much. I'm adopted. That's all I know, really.'

Avril nods. 'We know about your adoption. We actually placed you with your family when your parents died. But we lost track of them. And of you. It's only since we've felt the change start in you that we've been able to find you again.'

'The change? What does that mean?' The words are out of my mouth before they have a chance to register in my brain. I look at Josh to check he's okay with me asking questions, but he isn't looking at me—he's watching the others like he's waiting for a clue. Or to have his suspicions confirmed.

Peter looks at Tom, who nods. A silent agreement.

'Joshua, there's no easy way to say this but to put it simply, you aren't human.'

I know what I saw at Josh's place two nights ago. I know he didn't look human. But to have it confirmed so dryly—so easily, despite what Tom said—makes my brain go into a confusing whirl of thoughts. Josh's grip on my hand tightens and that's what I try to focus on. His fingers around mine, pressing, gripping. Needing me.

'Not human?' His voice cracks at the last word.

Tom shakes his head. 'No.'

'What am I then?' Josh's words are raspy, like his throat doesn't want to let the question out.

'You're part of an alien race. Part of our race. We're called Tagmires.'

The laugh spills out of me before I can stop it, and I cover my mouth with my hand, trying to pull myself together. The others are frowning at me and I shake my head, feeling light and stupid and nervous. This can't be true. How can this be true?

'I'm sorry. It's just... an alien race? Really? It feels like I'm on x-files or something?'

Peter nods like I haven't just insulted him.

'Yes, I can understand you might be sceptical. It doesn't change the fact that it's the truth. Perhaps a demonstration is needed.'

Josh's eyes widen and he sits forward in the chair. He needs this, that much is evident. I'm not sure I do but I decided to be here. And I'm not a coward.

There's a sharp crack, the noise echoing around the room, and the slight smell of sulphur, like a match being struck.

'Holy shit!' I scoot back in the chair, unable to help myself.

Because Peter's no longer standing in front of us. He's been replaced by... well, by something—someone—different. My breathing sounds as quick as Josh's. And he doesn't look any calmer than me. The creature...person...in front of us is tall. Well over seven-foot. And blue. A light blue—almost like it's a shimmer around his skin, rather than an actual skin colour. The same as Josh's had been. Otherworldly.

Alien.

His body still looks humanish—like a human on a major dose of steroids, anyway. Still two arms and two legs but muscles that look like they have no give in the skin at all. No softness.

And then, like I'm seeing things, Peter is back to...his human form, I guess. He takes one deep breath, like he's settling back into this body, and looks at Josh.

'This is what you are.'

Josh shakes his head slowly, like his brain can't quite believe what he saw.

'I...' he starts and then stops. Looking at me. I squeeze his hand and he starts again. 'I don't know what to say. How to understand this? What... why... I mean, if we're aliens, why are we here? On Earth? And what happened to my real parents?'

Peter sits in his chair, taking a moment to straighten his shirt. Making Josh wait. I want to punch him.

'That's difficult to answer as well. There's lots of political and cultural history tied up in that question. And we will tell you if you want to know. Essentially, we came here as refugees, escaping persecution and death.'

'And what about my parents?'

Avril sighs. 'Your father was killed before we got here. Taken and murdered as we were fleeing. Your mother... she was strong, Joshua, but she was so lost without your father. So lost. She tried hard to make a new life here, with you. But I don't think she ever really came back to us, emotionally. She died just after your third birthday.'

I can see the pain in Josh's eyes from the knowledge that he'll never meet his family, something he's dreamt of since he knew he was adopted. I want to take the grief from him, draw it out and throw it away, hold him until he feels okay. Protect him from it. Even though I know that's not possible.

'What about Joyce and Ray? Who are they? Are they... Tagmires too?' He's looking at Avril but it's Peter who answers.

'No. They're humans who first helped us settle here. One of our contacts, if you like. They offered to take you when your mother died and it seemed like a good option. One that would help you assimilate into human life – have a chance at a more normal childhood on our new home planet.'

'So they know about me? They know I'm different?'

Peter's eyes narrow, like he can feel the challenge in Josh's voice.

'Yes. They know. But we asked them to not tell you.

Not until the change started happening. There was a chance it may not have, given you'd only been on our planet for not even a year of your life. We didn't know if that would affect your ability to change.'

'And did you know what type of people they were when you gave me to them? Do you know how they've treated me?' Josh is shaking and I can feel the tenseness in his whole body. It matches mine.

I watch Avril, Peter, and Tom look at each other, and the answer is clear in their expressions. They knew. They knew about Joyce's instability. And Ray's rage. They knew and left him with them anyway. I feel like I want to throw up, nausea rising in my throat, burning, and I close my eyes for a second, swallowing it back down, trying to focus.

Josh is still, his jaw clenched, his hands in fists. And then he is up, out of the chair, racing outside.

Chapter Three

I run after him but Tom is quicker than I am. He stands in front of me, stopping me at the entrance to the hall.

'Get out of my way!' The anger is clear in my voice, but he ignores me.

'He has to acknowledge what he is and complete the change. It's important that he lets us help him.'

'Get out of my way!'

He grips my arm, his fingers tight on my skin.

'You don't understand. It can be dangerous if he doesn't let us help. He might hurt himself. Or you.'

I shake my head, refusing to believe the words. Even if there's a small—really small; tiny; minuscule—part of my brain that wonders if that might be possible. The small part that remembers the door and what he did. This is Josh. The boy I love. He'd never hurt me. Never.

I push past Tom, reefing my arm out of his grasp, and run.

'Please. He needs our help! It'll be worse at night. Harder to control.' Tom's words chase me down the hallway.

And then I'm outside, breathing in the sharp night air. I don't have to run far. Josh is five hundred metres away, standing in the middle of the road, panting like he's run ten kilometres. My heart is racing when I see him. Not because I'm scared. It's more that I hate to see him like this. Panicked. Confused.

He startles when I put my hand on his arm, like he hadn't even realised I was there. And then he grabs me, wrapping me in a hug so tight I can feel his desperation.

'It's okay,' I say, even though I know it's not. 'It'll be okay.'

I stroke my hands over his back, up and down, slow and rhythmic, until I can feel his body relax slightly. Enough that I think he's okay. As okay as he can be, given what he's learned tonight.

'Come on.' I move my hand, running it down his arm until I touch his fingers. 'Let's go back to your place.'

He nods but that's the only reaction I get on the way back to his house. Well, to the shed out the back that Joyce and Ray moved him into three years ago. And only because it meant they didn't have to interact with him. Didn't have to see him.

There's a new door to his room, unpainted and stark. It looks like a fresh scar, and my chest, my stomach, my head, ache for him, wanting to make this better. Wanting to take away all of this shit that's happening to him. None of which he's asked for. None of which he deserves.

We sit on his old red couch and he pulls me onto his lap. I tuck my head between his shoulder and neck and we sit there for a while, not talking, just breathing. Finally, his words come, full of emotion. 'Can you stay?'

I nod. Mum's been okay with us staying at each other's house for the last year, as long as it's not a school night.

Which is laughable really, given she's not there most nights to check. It's something that drew us together in the first place. Something to thank our shitty parents for. I text her anyway. She might be interested.

Turning slightly, I touch his face, my fingers lingering on his cheek, trying not to let my thoughts wander to how his skin looked during the change.

'Are you okay?'

He sighs and leans into my hand, closing his eyes for a moment.

'I don't know.'

'What can I do?'

'Being here is enough. I didn't think you'd want to be near me. Especially after seeing ... that. What Peter did. What I did.' He touches my lips, tracing the curve of them gently. 'Is that what I looked like? When you saw me?'

'Sort of. You were a little smaller, maybe.' I take a breath in, holding it for a second. 'How come you didn't tell me it was happening to you? Before I saw you?'

He gives a harsh laugh. 'How could I, when I didn't even know what the hell was going on myself? You would've thought I was nuts. I thought I was nuts!'

I can see his point. But still...

'You could've shown me.'

He shakes his head. 'I can't control it and I don't know when it's going to happen. Except it seems to happen at night, rather than during the day. So far, anyway.'

He moves, laying down on the couch and I lie next to him, curled up around his body, my legs over his, our faces close. I can see the lighter flecks of blue in his eyes. Eyes that feel almost as familiar as my own when I look at them. Eyes I trust.

'What about what Peter said to you?'

'I don't know. It seems so … unbelievable. Like I'm in a sci-fi movie or something. How can that be real? How could I not know anything about this? Feel different before all this started happening?'

I place my hand against his chest. 'Do you remember anything before Joyce and Ray? Your mum?'

He shakes his head. 'Nothing. I wish I could. I wish I knew what she looked like. What she sounded like…'

'Peter and Tom and Avril—they seemed to know her. They could tell you. Maybe they've got a photo or something.' My words are soft; hesitant. I don't want him to go back there; don't want him to have anything to do with them, given that they knew about Joyce and Ray, but that's not my call to make. His body is tense, but he stays quiet and when I look up at his face, he's staring at the ceiling.

'I don't know. I want to know about her. And my dad. But they left me with Joyce and Ray, even though they knew what sort of people they were. And they obviously didn't try too hard to find me.'

'What about the change?'

He closes his eyes then and when he talks, he sounds tired. Tired and overwhelmed and sad. 'At the moment, I don't care. I want to forget all about it. I don't want to be different—I've spent my whole life feeling like an outcast because of Joyce and Ray. And then you came along and I felt like I fitted in somewhere. I just want to stay here. You and me. Does that sound stupid?'

I put my head on his chest, hearing the thump of his heart under my ear. Whatever else is happening, whatever else is different, I love him. Whatever he is.

'No,' I say. 'That doesn't sound stupid.'

We spend the rest of the night in each other's arms.

And he doesn't change.

Chapter Four

When I wake in the morning, Josh is already up. He's even gone and bought coffee—a mocha for me, double shot, just the way I like it. I inhale the glorious aroma before sipping it. For a moment, I feel light. Happy. And then it all comes back to me and I don't know how to feel.

I watch him carefully and he smiles when he meets my eyes.

'I'm okay.'

'You sure?'

He comes over and bends down, kissing me gently on the lips, tasting me, teasing me. I wrap my hand around the back of his head and pull him closer, deepening our kiss. He chuckles as he pulls away, hand going through his hair.

'Even better now.'

I grin up at him. 'Well, okay then. Glad I could be of assistance.'

If he wants to ignore all of what's going on for the moment, who am I to make him talk about it?

'I was thinking we should have some fun today. Celebrate the weekend.'

I stand up, tugging at my shirt. 'I'm in. But I need to change first. Can we swing past my place?'

'Sure.'

We're quiet as we leave Josh's shed—not because Joyce and Ray would care about me being here — more so we don't have to deal with whatever mood they're in.

There's no one at home when I get there. God knows if Mum even read my message. Although, since I wasn't inundated by a million texts at two in the morning, asking where I was, I guess she must've. Either that or she never came home herself and has no idea I was out. I change my clothes, feed our cat, and put a load of clothes on to wash before we go. Some days, I feel more like the parent in my relationship with my mum. But she makes sure the rent is always paid, so I guess that's something.

Josh hugs me tight as we leave and I'm thankful for his solidness. His warmth. It's not only him who feels like he finally has somewhere he belongs.

We spend the day together doing not much—laying on the grass in the park and looking at clouds, eating hot chips and gravy while we people-watch, trying to guess their names, walking along the beach, collecting bits of driftwood. Kissing. Hugging. Touching.

It's perfect.

There are even moments in the day when I don't think about Josh's history and what it might all mean.

It's not until we're at his door that it comes back, slamming us in the face.

Joyce is there, waiting for us, running her hands through her hair over and over, like she's trying to pull it from her head.

'Hey, Joyce.' Josh positions himself in front of me, blocking her, and there's a hesitation in his voice. I know how he feels—Joyce's behaviour can be so erratic you never know what you're going to get. I put my hand on his shoulder, supporting him even if he doesn't need it.

'Has it happened?' She comes closer, sniffing his shirt like she's a dog looking for drugs. 'Has it? Tell me!'

He puts his hand up, pushing her back slightly. 'What, Joyce?'

'The change. The change! Has it happened? Are you definitely one of them?'

I feel everything in my body stop for a moment—my brain, my heart—everything. I can't believe she's asked him. That she's admitting she knows and has never said anything to him before. Never prepared him, never told him about his parents. I want to move forward, push her back, get her away from him, but Josh seems to know what I'm thinking and he puts his arm out, holding me back. And I know I need to let him do this.

'Do you mean the fact I'm an alien.' His voice is flat.

'Yes. Yes! I need to know if you're changing.'

'Why?'

She leans forward, her eyes looking everywhere but at him, jumping around like she can't find anything to focus on.

'I need you to take me back your planet,' she whispers. 'I need to get away. That's why we said we'd have you when you were a kid. So, when you were ready, you could take us.'

'I'm not going anywhere, Joyce.'

She grabs his shirt, clutching the collar in her fist, her face suddenly ugly.

'You little bastard. After all we've done for you.'

'All you've done! What have you done, except to make

sure I've got a roof and food, and even that hasn't been great?'

'That was enough. What more do you want?'

He wrenches his shirt out of her grasp and glares at her.

'How about some love? How about feeling like I wasn't some weirdo who didn't deserve to be loved by you?'

She stands tall, taking a step back. 'But we don't love you. How can we? You're not even human.'

That statement is so terrible, I can't stop the gasp the escapes me. I think it's that sound which makes her focus on me, her eyes hard as she looks me up and down.

'And you, you little slut, I know what you do. Staying over all the time. I bet you won't now you know he's not human.'

I narrow my eyes, ready to let her have it, the words sitting on my tongue. But they don't get a chance to come out. Because Josh is shaking beside me, a growl in his throat that's deep and guttural. And his skin is a flickering blue.

I touch his arm, getting his attention. His eyes are still blue—still Josh's eyes—and I can see the fear in them.

'Help me, Sar.' His voice is rough, like he's only just keeping the fear at bay.

Joyce is grinning manically beside me and she claps her hands, like she's watching a frigging circus, staged just for her. I've never hated someone so much in my life.

'This is it. This is the change, isn't it? You'll be able to take us. Get us away from here.'

I slap her, lashing out without thinking. The sound echoes in the cool night air and I can feel the sting on my hand where it connected with her cheek. Her eyes widen as she looks at me, the red mark on her face stark against her pale skin.

'Go.' I say, but it takes a yell to get her moving. 'Piss off!'

She scurries inside the house, slamming the door behind her. I don't know what she's going to do and frankly, I don't care. As long as it doesn't hurt Josh. I grab the key from where he's dropped it on the path. It takes three attempts for my shaking fingers to get it in the lock and then, finally, we're inside. Josh's tremors haven't stopped. If anything, they're worse, and his skin keeps flickering blue, like a neon light trying to turn on.

'Josh. It's okay. It's okay,' I say, touching his face, his neck. But he doesn't hear me. The anger is taking over. And I don't know what to do. I don't know how to help. Except to call Peter.

Chapter Five

I'm outside Josh's door, pacing up and down. Waiting. Worrying. My breath feels like it's only just getting into my lungs before being pushed out and I want to run. But I can't. I won't. Josh might need me.

Peter, Avril, and Tom are inside with him and I can hear them murmuring, their voices low and soft, interspersed by things being broken and Josh's growling. His roaring.

And his sounds of pain.

Each one tears at my heart, ripping little strips off until it feels like a raw mess.

They won't let me inside to help him. Avril stayed outside for a few moments with me when they first got here, to tell me they were going to help him through the change. That he might be dangerous—hurt me without even realising it—and that I needed to stay out, no matter what I heard. I'm not doing it for her. I'm doing it for Josh, because I know if he did accidentally hurt me, he'd never forgive himself.

When I asked what would happen if they couldn't help

him, her lips had tightened. But I'd pushed, wanting to know, needing to prepare myself. And she told me if they couldn't help him through the change, they'd have to take him away. Take him away and keep him locked up. Forever maybe. To keep him safe. To keep everyone safe.

Which is such shit. This is Joshua. My Josh. The boy who could never hurt anyone.

I can't do this anymore. I can't. Adrenalin infects my body, filling me up, wanting to burst out of my skin. My hand is on the door handle when something thumps against it, making it shake. I hesitate, thoughts filled with uncertainty as I hear Josh growl, the sound carrying clearly through the wood.

'Josh.' I put my hand against the door and even though my voice is soft, he hears me.

'Serena. Help me.' His pain and sadness are so clear, I turn the handle, hesitation gone, but the resistance takes me surprise, even though it shouldn't. Of course, they've locked it.

I pound on the door with my fist. 'Let me in. Unlock the door!'

But there's no answer. And the door stays locked. I pound again, ignoring the pain in my hand. 'Peter! Avril! Please!'

The frustration, the helplessness, fills me up, overflowing as tears. I wipe them away, my movements rough. I don't have time for this. Josh doesn't have time for this. My need to get to him, to help him, is choking me, making it hard to breathe, to think. I slam the door once more with my palm and then look around, trying to come up with a plan.

Racing around the back of the shed, I try the window at

the side. It's locked and the curtain is drawn, blocking my view of the room beyond. Shit. Shit!

My last hope—the window to the bathroom—is further along and I run to it, pulling on the latch. It opens! I don't stop to enjoy the relief coursing through me, pulling myself up through the window instead, falling through it and reefing my shoulder as I land on the floor. It doesn't matter; I don't care. I pull the bathroom door open and stop, staring at the scene in front of me.

It doesn't look like there's a piece of furniture still in one piece — the whole room is trashed. But that's not what makes my heart plummet, crashing down like it's no longer attached to my chest.

It's the fact that Peter, Tom, and Avril are surrounding Josh in their changed forms. And one of them is pointing a gun at him.

I race at them, but one of them catches me as I get closer, their arm closing around my waist. There's no way out. Their muscles are like iron, holding me still.

'No, Serena, you can't. He's not safe.' The voice is Avril's, but I don't look at her. I watch Josh. They've backed him into a corner, and his chest is heaving, rage and pain contorting his face. His skin looks like it's pulsing, the blue flaring with each breath.

'What's wrong? What's happening?' I have to force the words out of my mouth, fear making it difficult to talk. Not fear of Josh, even when he looks like this. But fear *for* him. Of what they're going to do to him. Of what that gun means.

'He's stuck in the change,' Avril says. 'It has to happen— it is happening—but he's fighting it. It doesn't help that he was angry when it started.'

I struggle in her arms. 'Let me go to him.'

'No!' Her arms tighten further around me. 'It's not safe, Serena.'

Josh growls again and goes to step forward, stopped when whichever man is holding the gun jabs it into him. Anger grabs my heart.

'Don't hurt him, you bastard!'

The one without the gun looks at me, his eyes hard. Peter, I think. Then he nods.

'Let her go.'

I can hardly believe it but, after a second of hesitation, Avril's arm loosens around me and I surge forward, breaking away, and then stop, a step away from Josh. I want to reach out, I want to touch him but now we're face to face, I don't know what I can do. How I can help. Will touching him hurt him? Does he need space?

He's quiet—well, quieter — but I can still see the anger and pain and fear in his face. I know he doesn't want to be different. I know it's fear holding him back.

And I understand what I need to do.

I take the last step, reaching out to touch his cheek with my hand. My heart's pumping so hard in my chest, it feels like the space is too small for it, and I wait to see what he'll do. I can see Josh in his eyes. He's there.

His skin is softer than it looks, his jaw squarer, everything about him hard angles, like he's made from marble. There's a beauty to this form that he's fighting—a magnificence. My hand traces the line of his cheek, down his neck, to his chest. I lay my palm on his skin, where his heart is. Was? I've got no idea about any of this except that I know this is Josh still. And I love him. The blue light on my skin making it look like I'm changing too.

Maybe I am.

'Josh.' My voice is soft and I hope he can hear the love in it. The love for him, whatever his form is.

'Serena.' His voice is still raspy, harsh, but I smile at him. He knows me. I haven't lost him. He is still Josh.

I reach up, hand at the back of his head, pulling him down. He lets me do it. And then, his lips are on mine, softer than I thought they'd be. I kiss him gently, one small one after another, layering them, until he kisses me back, his hand going around me, pulling me closer.

'I love you,' I say between kisses. 'Whatever you look like. Whatever you are. You're mine. My Josh. I love you.'

'I can't do it,' he says. 'I can't!'

I kiss him again. 'Yes, you can. I want you to. Please.'

I feel the shudder go through his body and pull back slightly, watching him.

'Change for me.'

His eyes search my face like he's trying to find the lie in my words. I hold my breath...

A sharp crack fills the room, the same one we heard when Peter changed, and Josh stands in front of me, the change complete, the blue of his skin consistent. He's panting like he's run a marathon, but the anger and pain are no longer on his face.

He reaches out a large hand—so big it cradles half my head. I lean into his touch, loving the strength I feel in him.

'Serena,' he says, and even though his voice is different, his body is different, I can feel the love in his voice. For me.

And, while I don't know what any of this means for us—for our future—in the end, our love is all that matters. It's the only thing that's ever mattered.

I don't realise the others have left until I hear the door shut and when I turn back to Josh, he's watching me, eyes serious.

'Are you okay?'

I shrug. 'As long as you're okay, I'm okay.'

He shakes his head. 'I mean with this.' He gestures to his body and to the blue of his skin. 'I'm so different, Ser. Weird. Can you love this?'

I touch my hand to his cheek and then arch an eyebrow. 'What's not to love? You'll make a hell of a reading light.'

His laugh is all I need to know that we'll make this work. Whatever it looks like.

Adventure Seeking Goddess

Week 1

'How can an empty wardrobe be so devastating and yet be such a relief at the same time?'

Sam, best friend, sympathiser and bringer of ice-cream, waved her spoon in the air.

'It's because you were ready for it to end, even if you didn't want to acknowledge it. You and Simon haven't been good for a while. You know this.'

I sighed. 'I know. I *know*. But it seems so final. Five years of my life just...pfft. Like it never existed. I wanted to marry him.'

Sam snorted and I frowned at her.

'What? I did!'

'No, you didn't,' she said with what felt like an insulting level of assuredness. 'You thought you *should* marry him, since you'd been together so long, but you didn't really want to.'

I paused, spoon half buried in the ice-cream she'd brought, and looked out over my view of the park—the whole reason I'd bought the unit despite its seventies-entrenched brown and olive interior. The home Simon and I were going to make together; although, apparently, that had only been my dream. His dream, so he informed me as he left my life, was to travel to Alaska and become a world-famous environmental photographer.

It'd come as a bit of a shock really, given I'd had no idea he was into photography *or* the environment. I'd wanted to point out that I'd always been the one to take the recycling out, for God's sake, but it hadn't been worth the breath. He just would've given me that slightly sardonic look I'd grown to really hate in the last six months—the one that said he understood the world in a way he felt was beyond me.

'We're rooted in routine,' he'd said. 'I love you, Emma, but I need more. I need adventure and spontaneity. And I need to find it on my own.'

'But you're an accountant! You love routine.'

He'd touched my arm and I'd stepped back, out of his reach.

'I know this is hard and probably a bit unexpected but I need more and I think you do too. Are you happy—really?'

'Yes!' I'd said at the time but now, with Sam's words echoing in my brain, I wondered if I truly had been. Life with Simon had been...comfortable.

Predictable.

Stable.

Shit—he'd been right. We'd been rooted in routine; rotting in routine, really. And, if I was being honest, our love had been a part of that repetitiveness—something we did because we always had.

I sighed. 'You're right.'

'I know,' she said, raising one eyebrow and licking the ice-cream from her spoon. 'So, what now? It's been three months, Em. Time to shake it off. Unleash the divine, adventure-seeking Goddess I know is lurking inside you.'

'Adventure-seeking Goddess?' I laughed. 'I don't think I've ever been that.'

'Well, it's time then. You're twenty-eight, not eighty-eight. And you don't need to have your whole life planned out.' She pointed her spoon at me. 'Which is definitely you compensating for the fact that you were always more of an adult that your mum ever was.'

I rolled my eyes at her pop-psychology and finished scooping out some of the best-friend-in-crisis ice-cream she'd ever delivered. Even if there was some truth to what she was saying, I'd never admit it.

Had I been so busy being the responsible one all the time though, that I'd forgotten to have fun?

I absently put the spoon in my mouth, still thinking of Simon's words, and stopped, statue-still, as the flavours melted on my tongue.

'Sweet Jesus.' I pulled the tub closer to me. 'What is this, apart from orgasm on a spoon?'

Sam put another spoonful in her mouth before answering me, closing her eyes for a moment. 'I know, right? *Pina Colada*—my favourite so far. The fact I'm sharing this with you is testament to how much I love you. I found them last week—*Sweet Pleasures*. It's made locally.'

I filled my spoon again and let the deliciousness overwhelm my taste buds. Maybe it was the sugar hit or perhaps the hard-truth reflection, but it was time, I decided. Time for change.

I looked at Sam. 'I need your help.'

'Sure. What with?'

'I'm going to try to do something new, every week.

Something I've never done before. But I need you to keep me honest—make sure I do it.'

She grinned at me. 'Deal. And your reward each week shall be a new flavour of *Sweet Pleasures*.' She held up her spoon and I crossed my handle with hers to complete our pact. 'You're going to make an awesome adventure-seeking Goddess.'

Week 2

I t was impossible to sit on the grass without groaning on the way down. I had no idea how I was going to get back up but it didn't matter. That was future-Emma's problem. Right then, I needed to be in the park, surrounded by nature.

'Are you okay?'

The rich, masculine voice came from behind me and I spun as quickly as I could, which honestly wasn't that fast, to find the owner. He was perched in the low fork of a tree, book in hand, one leg swinging lazily, and warm coffee-coloured eyes looking at me with interest.

'Sorry?'

He smiled and a small part of me melted like chocolate in the sun.

'That sounded painful,' he said, closing the book on his index finger. 'I was just wondering if you were okay?'

My cheeks burned and I laughed. 'Yes. First week of Hula Fit. I wasn't expecting it to be quite as hard on my body.'

'Hula Fit?'

'Exercise with a hula hoop.'

'Ah.' There was something in the silence after this calm acceptance that made me want to keep talking—not to fill the space but because it felt...comfortable. Helped by the fact maybe that he was a stranger.

'This week was my test run. I don't think I'll be heading back.'

'You like to try new things?'

I leant back, legs out in front of me. 'Not usually but I've decided it's time for new adventures.'

He acknowledged that with a nod and slipped down out of the tree, sinking athletically to the ground without groaning—show-off!—before leaning back against the tree trunk. Objectively, he was gorgeous. Dark blond hair that just called for fingers to be run through it, a dimple in his left cheek and a white buttoned-up shirt with rolled-up sleeves that showed off wide shoulders and toned arms. But somehow, the fact he was holding a book made him even more attractive.

'And is this your first new adventure?'

I realised, with blush-inducing mortification, that I'd been ogling his chest and had no idea what he'd asked. 'Um, yes?'

He cocked his head. 'So, this is your first adventure?'

'Oh,' I said, brain rushing to keep up. 'Yes, this was my first. I mean, not my first, obviously, because I've tried new things before but it's my first this time. An adventure virgin, if you like.' Oh my god, why had I said that! Especially when it made no sense! Shit. Stop, Emma. But the words kept babbling out. 'It was my friend's idea—Sam. She's buying me ice-cream each week as an incentive. *Sweet Pleasures*. That's what the ice-cream's called, I mean, not what...'

Finally, the words petered out.

He chuckled and a fizz of attraction travelled over my skin, making me smile with him. 'Yes, I've heard of the brand—my sister's a fan. Have you got a favourite flavour?'

'I've only had one—*Pina Colada*. Heaven on a spoon. We're trying another one tonight.'

'Heaven on a spoon? I'll have to try it.' He smiled at me and the heat intensified on my skin. I hadn't blushed this much since high school. 'Have you decided on your next adventure?'

I licked my lips, mouth suddenly dry, and took a deep breath. 'Roller derby.' I couldn't believe I was telling him this, not when I wasn't sure yet that I was actually brave enough to follow through.

He lips quirked in a way that made it hard to look away. 'Wow, that's adventurous. Can you skate?'

'Sure.' I leant forward again, dusting off my hands, trying to look unconcerned at the fact I hadn't skated for fifteen years. It couldn't be that hard, surely—like riding a bike. 'It's just trials so shouldn't be as full on as a game. And it's something I've never tried.'

'Can I recommend the *Chocolate Jewel* ice-cream then, as your reward for being so adventurous? It's brownie, raspberry swirl—my sister's favourite.'

'Sounds delicious.' I sighed and looked around at the fading light. 'Well, I suppose I need to find a way to get up and head home.'

He stood, holding out his hand. 'Allow me to be of assistance.'

I wondered later if it was weird that I hadn't even hesitated. My hand felt small in his and when he pulled me up, I was close enough to see the gold flecks in his eyes. It made me strangely breathless—a flurry of warmth and promise. And when, after a few beats, our hands dropped apart, disappointment flooded through me.

'I'm Ben, by the way.' He hadn't moved back and neither had I.

'Emma.'

'Emma,' he said, as if my name tasted good in his mouth. 'Enjoy your *Sweet Pleasures*.'

Week 3

Ben was reading in the tree again. I'd told myself I just wanted a walk in the park but honestly, I was hoping he'd be there. I'd been thinking about him all week—his eyes, his hands, the way he'd said my name...

As if he was waiting for me too, or maybe I was totally deluding myself, he closed his book as soon as he saw me and smiled.

'How did you survive roller derby?'

He winced as I showed him the bruises on my leg. 'Ouch. And are you going back?'

I shook my head. 'Definitely not. You should see the rest of my body—it's covered in bruises.' And then I realised what I'd said and could feel the heat on my chest, burning its way up my neck, my face.

His mouth quirked. 'I'm not averse to the idea if you wanted to show me.'

My heart loudly signalled its agreement in morse code and I put my hand to my chest, trying to calm it.

'What flavour ice-cream did you get?'

I swallowed past the tightness in my throat. '*Mediterranean Bliss*—honey pistachio.'

He nodded. 'Interesting combination. What did you think?'

I walked closer, leaning against the branch he was sitting on. Under the canopy of rich, green leaves, it felt like our own little world.

'Amazing. But *Pina Colada* is still my favourite.'

'A woman who's sure of what she enjoys. I like that.'

Every organ in my body clenched at the look in his eyes, the tone of his voice, and I had to stop myself stepping closer to him—pulled like metal to a magnet.

'Do you always sit in a tree to read?'

He laughed, but ran his hand self-consciously through his hair. 'Not always. But there's something...comforting about it. I used to do it as a kid and decided I needed to start again.'

I tilted my head. 'Why?'

'There's been a lot of change in my life the last six months, including starting a new business. I needed to go back to some of the things I knew I enjoyed—things that brought me pleasure. So, reading in a tree was one of them.'

I liked that—the synchronicity of where we both were.

'And how are you going with the changes?'

A small smile graced his lips—there and gone—like a portent to a mystery I'd be happy to get to the bottom of. 'Getting easier all the time. What do you do when you're not having new adventures?'

'Interior design.'

'Do you enjoy it?'

I hesitated for a moment and then decided to tell the truth. It seemed easy to do that with him. 'Yes, mostly. Although it's been recently pointed out to me that I have both a wide responsibility streak and a planning fixation, which probably makes me good at my job but doesn't work so well in other areas of my life. Hence, the need to explore becoming an adventure-seeking Goddess.'

He chuckled, leaning forward along the branch, closer to me. 'An adventure-seeking Goddess. That suits you.'

A lightness filled my soul, which was ridiculous. He knew nothing about me. And yet, it was nice to be thought of as something more than the responsible one. Even Simon had seen me as that — always happy for me to fulfil that role, although that's what seemed to have driven him away in the end.

'I'm trying,' I said and it felt, in that moment, like I might be able to get there.

'What's on the agenda for this week's adventure?'

I frowned. 'I'm not sure. Honestly, something that doesn't make my body feel like it's being tortured would be good.'

'Does reading in a tree count as an adventure or is that too tame?'

My heart tripped over itself before beating faster as if to make up for the mistake.

'That sounds wonderful.' And although I tried to keep my tone light, even I could hear the slight breathlessness to it.

'Next week? Same time, same place?'

And when I nodded, it felt like something bigger.

Week 4

E xcitement and nervousness warred in my body, creating a jitteriness deep in my bones—as if I couldn't even walk properly, let alone climb a tree. I gripped the book I'd bought and marched determinedly across the park. I didn't know what to expect—how to plan or control this—and it was equal parts terrifying and wonderful.

Ben was waiting for me in the tree, as he had been for the last two weeks, and I smiled at him, even though it felt stretched and weird. He reached down, his long fingers wrapping around mine as he helped me up, the muscles in his arms bunching in a way that made me want to wrap my hand around them.

He'd moved further up the branch, leaving me to sit snugly in the fork of the tree.

'I've taken your spot.'

The twist of his mouth inspired the same movement in my stomach. 'I'm happy to give it up.'

'Oh,' I said, unable to look away from those perfect lips. 'Okay. Thanks.'

He smiled, and my stomach did an extra twist for good measure. 'Absolutely my pleasure.'

I cleared my throat, totally out of my depth. 'What now?'

'Now, we read.'

'Right, of course.' I opened my book—one I'd been meaning to read for ages—but the words may as well have been written in a different language for all the sense they made. I was distracted by the barest distance between his leg and mine; the thought that if I just moved slightly, our bodies would touch; the sound of his breathing; the smell of him.

When I'd read the same paragraph three times and still didn't know what it said, I looked up. He wasn't even pretending to read—his deliciously brown eyes were watching me and the jolt of desire that brought felt like it was almost big enough to knock me out of the tree.

'You're not reading.' The desire flavoured my tone.

He tilted his head slightly. 'I thought I wanted things that brought me happiness in the past, but it turns out new possibilities of pleasure are much more enthralling.'

'Almost like a new adventure,' I said, my voice just above a whisper.

'Exactly like that,' he said, and he leant forward, giving me plenty of time to say no or turn my head. But I did neither. Instead, I leant forward too.

His lips touched mine, whisper soft—a teasing taste. Then firmer, more insistent, although I wasn't sure if that was him or me. I breathed into the kiss, my lips parting slightly and his tongue slid against mine, as if he was savouring the flavour of me. His hand cupped the side of my jaw, tracing the line of it, following the curve of my neck, my nerve endings anticipating every touch. I was addictively overwhelmed by him—his touch, his smell, his taste. So much so that when he pulled back, I forgot for a moment where I was. There was just him.

We sat in silence, looking at each other, our hands entwined.

'I like reading in trees,' I said and thrilled at the fact I could make him laugh.

'I bought you something.' He reached further up the tree, to a cooler bag I hadn't noticed wedged in another fork. 'Ice-cream. *Sweet Pleasures*, in fact.'

I licked my lips and it had nothing to do with the thought of ice-cream and everything to do with the remembered taste of his lips.

'Oh. Have I convinced you to try it?'

He didn't answer, instead taking the lid off the container and digging a spoon in. He held it out to me, his eyes daring me to taste. With deliberate slowness, in a way that made me feel decidedly Goddess-like, I took the spoon in my mouth, the sweetness dissolving on my tongue.

His small intake of breath made me feel...adventurous.

'Zesty lime and raspberry,' he said, as if the words had to fight their way out of a tight chest.

'Delicious.'

'Yes,' he said, but he wasn't looking at the ice-cream. 'Inspired by you.'

I'm sure my confusion showed through my smile. 'What?'

'*Sweet Pleasures*,' he said. 'It's my company. The changes I've had in the last six months.'

I laughed. 'Really?'

He nodded and took the paper bag from around the tub, displaying the name. *Adventure-seeking Goddess*.

And it felt like I was.

Booked for Murder

Chapter 1

My life is defined by secrets.

Hearing them, keeping them, using them when I need to.

Which isn't often—I try to use my telepath powers for good but sometimes, people are shitheads and need to be taught a lesson.

Pushing open the door to the coffee house, I stop for a moment, shutting my eyes against the onslaught of thoughts from others in the shop, letting them wash over me, surround me, fill me, until it feels like I can't hear my own thoughts over the top of everyone else's.

Taking a deep breath, I let it all settle into the back of my mind—a constant noise like background traffic. Except when people yell their thoughts, which is usually, for some weird reason, their secrets. They're hard to keep out.

I open my eyes and move into the cafe, passing two women having coffee. They're friends, I think, although the one with the dark hair knows it'd destroy the blond if she found out she was sleeping with her husband. Like I said, shitheads. She's lucky I'm in a good mood.

Liz, the owner, smiles as I walk up to the counter.

"Hey Bree, caramel latte, double shot?"

I nod, mouth already salivating at the thought of the caramelly, caffeine goodness. My one weakness. Every morning, I take a break from my graphic design business to wander down for my fix. I could've paid for my own machine with the money I'd spent but, if I didn't do this, I'd probably never leave my unit. I'd just stay there like a hermit up the mountain, alone, and free from other people's thoughts.

When I move back from the counter, I notice the new barista for the first time. He's cute. Curly brown hair, broad shoulders and arms that show nice definition. Arms I'm obviously staring at too long because I realise he's stopped moving and is grinning at me.

I can feel the heat on my cheeks but I don't return the smile. Dating when you can hear the guy's every thought sucks. There's something very, *very* off-putting hearing their internal dialogue about everything you do, every doubt they have and everything they want to do later.

And that's when it hits me, like the proverbial ton of bricks.

I can't hear him.

Nothing!

I'm so stunned I just stand there, staring at him, not registering that he's calling my name until it must be the third or fourth time. I jolt forward, feeling like an idiot, but too amazed to give into that feeling. This has never happened before. Ever.

"Bree?" He's holding the cup out to me, smile still there but slightly smaller, like he can't work out what my problem is. At least, I think that's what it is. Even though I hate it most of the time, I suddenly feel like I'm working blind, not knowing how to react without his thoughts to guide me.

"Yes, thanks." I reach out to take it. "Sorry, daydreaming."

The smile is back. "Was it about me?"

My laugh startles me. "Sure, if that'll help you sleep better tonight."

Look at me – flirting! I almost feel...normal.

"I'm Oliver."

"Bree." I groan inwardly. God, I suck at this. "But you already know that."

"Sounds much better when you say it though. Bree." He says it softly, like a caress and I want to tell him he's wrong – I'd much rather hear him say it again but I don't. I can't bring myself to leave though, so I stand there awkwardly, taking a sip from my cup, really wishing that, for once, I'd ordered in.

I want to know why I can't hear him. I can still hear everyone else's thoughts in the café. What's special about him?

"Are you new in town?" It's the only question I can think to ask that doesn't sound totally weird. Because, let's face it, *how come I can't read your mind* or *what's up with your brain* aren't great conversation starters.

He moves behind the machine to make the next order. "No, I'm in the second year of my social work degree. But I needed money, so here I am. What about you?"

"Graphic design. I mean, that's what I do."

"Cool." *I wonder if she'd go out with me?*

"Sorry, what?" My breath catches in my throat – the hope of a normal relationship draining out of me as quickly as it came.

"I said cool. That must be great."

But that's it – only the words from his mouth. No thoughts to accompany them. My head's spinning, hope springing up again, like it's on a frigging pogo-stick.

"Yeah, it is. Great, I mean."

He finishes the coffee and calls out to the person who ordered it. An older woman, hair slicked back into a tight bun.

Damn, he's cute. Wonder if he likes older women. The things I could let him do to me...

I slam down my shields quick, not wanting to even begin to know what she wants done to her. Well, not shields really – I wish it was that easy – but I start to sing in my head. Loudly. It's taken years and years of practice to be able to do that and still be able to hold a conversation.

"Enjoy." Oliver gives her a quick smile before turning back to me. Once again, none of his thoughts reach me. Total silence. And yet, I know that one random thought was his. It had to be.

He moves around the machine, coming to the other side of the counter, closer to me.

"Listen, I know this is probably weird since you've only met me, but would you like to go out for a drink later?"

There! See, it was his thought! I don't know if I smile because I'm right or because of the fact he's asking me out. Maybe a bit of both. And then I realise I still haven't answered him.

"That'd be great." And I'm not lying. The thought that I might be able to be with someone where I can't hear *every* thought has me almost giggling like a school girl. I can handle a random thought ever now and then. I mean, it's got to be better, doesn't it?

Chapter 2

Four months later

"Are you sure you're up for this? It's not too late to back out."

"Oh my God, will you stop? I'm getting paranoid." I shove at Oliver's shoulder as I get out of the car. "Don't you want me to meet your family? Is that it? Are you embarrassed by me?"

He laughs and throws an arm around my shoulder, pulling me into a hug.

"Are you kidding? Mum and Dad are going to love you. But you're meeting *all* of them today. I feel like I'm throwing you in the deep end and you're going to run for the hills, screaming, and I'll never see you again. Sometimes they can be... you know... intense."

I pull back slightly and look up at him.

"What do you mean intense?"

He rubs his hands up my bare arm and I try not to be distracted by his touch. "Well, since you're the first girl I've ever introduced them to, Mum will probably give you the third degree. Not in a horrible way but just because she's excited."

I smile at him. "I'm the first one?"

He leans down to kiss me, a sweet one that lingers for just a little more than it should.

"Don't let it go to your head." *God, she's amazing. I hope this doesn't scare her off.*

It's those little pops of thoughts that make my heart feel like it's glowing. I still don't know why his brain works differently—why, out of everyone in this world, I only get a few of his thoughts rather than the constant stream I get from others. But after four months of feeling like I'm almost a normal person in a normal relationship, I'm definitely not complaining.

"Never."

He wraps his fingers around mine. "Okay, let's do this."

I smooth a hand over my pulled back hair and then down the front of the dress I'd agonised over before I'd bought it last week, trying to make a good impression for Oliver's sister's wedding. Not too sexy but not too staid, feminine but not girly, elegant enough for a wedding but not like I was trying to get all the attention.

"You look beautiful," Oliver says and I squeeze his hand in response, trying to ignore the nervous flutters getting worse in my stomach. I'm just grateful it's an outdoor wedding. Being inside seems to make people's thoughts more intense—harder to block out—like they're echoing around the space rather than dispersing. A bit like sounds waves, I guess.

We stop at the start of the path leading down to the

gardens. I can see people milling down there, and can just hear the edge of their thoughts. Not that Oliver knows about my telepathy. God, I can't imagine how that conversation would even go, especially only four months into our relationship. I know, at some stage, I'll have to tell him...maybe... but essentially, I'm being a coward. All he knows is I don't like crowds.

"Are you okay?"

I take a deep breath and nod at him. I can do this—for him. For us.

It's when we're nearly at the end of the path, the thoughts already swirling around me, that a woman looks up and smiles at us. She's tiny but has her hair piled up onto her head like she's trying to give herself a few more inches of height. The man next to her looks so much like an older version of Oliver there's no denying these are his parents.

Oh God, here we go. I hope Oliver's new girlfriend is nice. Please don't let her be a bitch.

I smile at this mother's thoughts, pleased I'm not the only one freaking out. Oliver wraps his arm around my shoulders as we stop in front of them.

"Mum, Dad, this is Bree. Bree, this is Lara and Michael."

I nod at them, still smiling like an idiot, trying to filter out all the other thoughts around me and focus in on theirs while attempting to talk normally — something I've done all my life, but it's harder when I'm nervous.

"Hi. It's lovely to meet you. Thanks for letting me crash your daughter's wedding."

Lara takes one of my hands in hers and squeezes. "We were excited when Oliver said he was bringing someone. It's lovely to finally meet you." *She seems lovely. And thank God she's not dressed inappropriately.*

It's these thoughts I *like* being able to hear—the ones that make me feel like I've made good choices.

I turn to Michael and frown before I realise what I'm doing and hurriedly clear my face again. Because, just like Oliver, I realise I can't hear his thoughts. Is it a genetic thing maybe? Something about them that means they're 'immune' to my eavesdropping? I'm so excited by that thought I almost feel like dancing. Two people I can't hear!

"It's lovely to meet you," he says, a gentle smile on his face. "I hope we're not all too overwhelming today. It was brave of you to come, especially for the first introductions."

I laugh and shake my head. "Oliver's been trying to talk me out of it all morning."

"So, Bree, how did you and Oliver meet?" *He seems to be really taken with her. He hasn't let her go. I hope she fits in with us. Jane said her daughter-in-law is horrible and they never see their son anymore.*

"At the café where he works, actually."

"I swept her away with my awesome coffee and witty banter." Oliver winks down at me and I lean into him, trying to not react to his mother's delight that he seems so happy.

"Yep, although the coffee outweighed the banter by a fair bit."

"Hey!" Oliver said in mock outrage.

His father laughs and ushers us towards the chairs set out on the grass. "Oh, I think you're going to fit in fine. I'll see you all later—I'm going to get ready to escort Sarah down the aisle." *I can't believe this moment's actually here.*

With that sweet random thought of Michael's swirling in my brain, the next fifteen minutes are a blur of meetings—Oliver's grandmother, three aunts and two uncles, half a dozen cousins (one who was *not* a gentleman in his thoughts and who I was definitely going to stay away from) and some family friends. I'm singing by the end and already getting tired.

It's a relief then, when the music starts playing and Oliver's sister stands at the end of the aisle, her arm tucked into Michael's, and I can let the singing go.

And then I wished I hadn't.

Because a stray thought hits me. One that sounds like Michael's thought voice from before. But this one isn't as sweet.

How can I murder them so it'll look like an accident?

Chapter 3

I freeze, not knowing what to do with that thought, especially since there aren't any other follow-up thoughts to help me make sense of it. And when I look at Michael, he's gazing down proudly at Sarah.

Almost like the thought wasn't his. Maybe it wasn't.

Sure—that's it.

Except I know I'm lying to myself. I'm so used to hearing everyone's thought voice, it's exactly like listening to their speaking voice. I know it was Michael. I know he's thinking about killing someone. No, not someone. He said them. He's thinking about killing multiple people!

I spin around to face the front again, not able to look at him.

Oliver squeezes my hand. "You doing okay?"

I smile at him, even if it feels like a weak imitation of the real thing. "Sure. Just a bit of headache."

He wraps his arm around my shoulders and I lean into him, trying to work out what it means as Michael and Sarah walk down the aisle past us.

I hear none of the vows, pay no attention to the 'I do's',

ignore the thoughts of everyone in the tent without even really trying—Michael's words just spin round and round in my head, like a whirlpool sucking every other thought away.

I strain to hear another thought from his mind, anything that will help me make sense of it or help me know what he's planning. God, out of all the people in the world, why did he have to have the same warped brain as Oliver?

And then everyone is standing and clapping and smiling and I do it all on autopilot. Watch Michael and Lara give Sarah and her new husband a hug, share a joke with the groom's parents like everything in the world is normal and okay.

And maybe it is. Maybe it was just the shock of being happy not to hear Michael initially and then hearing his crazy words that's made this seem worse than it is. I mean, people think things all the time and don't act on them. I know that better than anyone! Yes, that's it. It must be.

I take a deep breath and follow everyone out of the tent, Oliver's fingers threaded through mine, making me feel grounded. He tugs me towards his sister.

"Sar, you look beautiful," he says, as he leans in to kiss her cheek.

"Not looking so bad yourself, little brother," she smiles up at him and then turns to me. "You must be Bree."

"Yes. Thanks so much for letting me crash your wedding."

"Don't be silly," she says, nudging Oliver's shoulder. "This guy's crazy about you; talking about Bree this and Bree that. I think he would've killed me if I hadn't invited you."

I laugh, even though it's forced. That's hitting a little close to the bone, really. I love the fact that Oliver's face has gone red though, and he gives me a sheepish grin.

"Christ, by the time we leave here, Bree's going to be thinking I'm a stalker or something."

I kiss him and the crowd around us wahoo.

They look like they're happy.

It's Sarah's thought and I want to tell her we are, but it would be a dead giveaway. And I don't need them to know I'm a freak. Not when they seem to like me.

I manage to enjoy myself during the reception. Michael's speech is everything I'd expect—loving and proud and there aren't any stray thoughts I don't want to hear. Just normal thoughts every now and then from him. It confirms that the thought was his though.

Oliver pulls me into a gentle embrace during the dancing and I snuggle into his chest, loving the fact that we fit together so well.

God, I love her. Holy shit. I love her!

I almost jolt in his arms as I hear his thoughts. He loves me? My heart feels like it's trying to burn a hole through my ribs and I hug him tighter, even though I can't tell him why. Except, perhaps I could. Maybe, if he loves me, he could hear about my telepathy and still want to be with me.

Lara and Michael twirl in a circle next to us, and Lara laughs as Michael dips her.

"How are you enjoying yourself, you two?" I can hear the happiness in Michael's voice as he looks at us.

"Good when I'm not being shown up by my father," Oliver says, suddenly twirling me and leaning into our own dip, which takes my breath away. I laugh as he brings me back up but the laughter dies on my lips.

I could use poison. A slow acting one no one could trace. Hemlock, maybe. I'll have to research it—find out where you could buy it and the best way to use it.

And I know I have to tell Oliver about his father.

Chapter 4

The hot water from the shower takes some of the tightness out of my shoulders but I still can't find the words to tell Oliver his father is a murderer. Well, a murderer in the making.

I dry off and wrap myself in my thick dressing gown—my comfort go-to; so much better than food—and head into the bedroom. Oliver's already in bed and he gives me a lazy smile as I sit on his side of the bed, wrapping his hand around my arm and bringing me down for a kiss. A very distracting one that almost makes me forget what I'm trying to do.

I push myself up off his chest and rub my eyebrow.

"Okay, what's wrong?"

I try for an innocent expression. "Why do you think something's wrong?"

"You rubbed your eyebrow. You always do that right before you tell me something you don't think I'll like."

"Wow, you're observant."

He shrugs. "We did non-verbal cues last semester. Come on, tell me."

Crap, I hope she's not breaking up with me. Was the wedding too much?

That's it—the chance to tell him—to prove to him what I can do.

I take a deep breath, hardly believing what I'm about to do. "No, the wedding wasn't too much. And I'm not breaking up with you."

As soon as the words are out, I want to stuff them back in my mouth. The panic blossoms in my chest like an exploding nuclear bomb and I think I'm going to be sick. The only other person in my life who knows what I can do is my mother, and she's made me pay for it my whole life.

"What?" Oliver's frowning at me and I shake my head, the panic taking me back to my usual coward status.

"Nothing. It doesn't matter." I can't do it. I can't take the chance he'll leave me.

"No, you said you weren't breaking up with me. Why would you say that?"

"I was being stupid. It didn't mean anything." I flutter my hands in the air, the panic clear in my voice now, and he grabs one and holds on to it.

"Hey, it's okay. Bree." He stops talking until I look into his eyes. Eyes that tell me I can trust him; that he's a good person, not like my mother, who used me and hated what I could do, all at the same time. "It's okay. You can tell me anything."

I lick my lips, my mouth so dry I'm not sure I can actually get the words out. But I need to do it—now or never.

"I said it because I knew that's what you were thinking."

He smiles, like there's nothing odd about that. "And how did you know that? What non-verbals do I have?"

I shake my head, not smiling back. "It's not non-verbals. I know because I heard your thoughts. I'm a telepath."

There. It's out. Out into the silence, sitting around us like a suffocating blanket.

He goes still. So still that I think, for a moment, he's actually stopped breathing.

"I'm a telepath," I say again. "I hear thoughts all the time and have for as long as I can remember."

"You hear thoughts?" He sounds like he's trying to believe me—trying to be supportive—but there's a part of him thinking he's sitting in an apartment with a crazy woman.

"Please don't hate me." My voice is so soft, it's a miracle he can hear me.

"I don't hate you. I'm just... shocked, I guess." He sits up in the bed, his back against the headrest. "Right. A telepath. Cool. Can you hear all my thoughts?"

I shake my head. "That's one of the things that attracted me to you in the first place. I can hear everyone else's thoughts—all of them, all the time—but with you, I don't get that. I only get a stray thought every now and then. Like the one you just had about not wanting me to break up with you."

I'm hoping that's still true but I don't say it, just in case.

He frowns. "Why don't you get all my thoughts like you do everyone else's?"

"I don't know. Your brain is just different, I guess."

"What do you mean? Broken or something?"

I snort. "You must be the only person who'd be more worried your brain is different rather than happy I can't hear all your thoughts."

He gives me a small smile. "Sorry. Just trying to wrap my head around of all of this. It's a lot to take in."

I nod, waiting to see what he says next.

"Can you... I mean, I'm trying to believe it—I really am, but it's totally not something I thought I'd ever have to deal with. Can you tell me something else I've thought?"

He wants proof. That's understandable, even if it hurts a tiny bit.

"Um, sure. You know when we were in the park last week and you saw the man yelling at the little kid because he'd run off without saying something. He reminded you of your friend, Chris."

He stares at me like the words are taking a while to sink into his brain.

"Shit." He rubs his forehead. "Is that why you get headaches and don't want to be in crowds? Because of all the thoughts?"

"Yeah, although over the years I've got better at tuning them out."

He shakes his head. "It must be really hard, to have all that information bombarding you all the time. And am I the only person who's mostly blocked from you?"

My heart beats faster in my chest again, like it's trying to thump out a warning. "No, your dad's the same."

"Huh. Well, it must be a genetic thing or something, hey? Maybe we're not broken. Maybe we're just special."

I laugh, but it sounds forced. "Yep, that must be it."

"Okay, what else is there? Something's still wrong."

I sit cross-legged on the bed and he must take it as a sign it's serious because he sits forward.

"When we were at the wedding, I heard some of your dad's thoughts."

"Okay..."

"And, you know, he had the usual thoughts about being

proud of Sarah and how beautiful she looked. He's proud of you too, by the way."

"Mm-hmm."

"And your mum—boy, she has lots of thoughts. She's really happy for both of you too and thinks I'll be good for you, so that's always nice to hear."

"Bree, you're really starting to freak me out, which is sort of weird given how quickly I've taken on the telepath thing. Just tell me, okay?"

"Yep. Okay. Sure." I take a deep breath and then rush the words out. "Your dad was thinking about murder."

He frowns. "What?"

"He was thinking about murdering someone. Well, a few people, by the sound of it. And making it look like an accident. He was wondering if poisoning would work and was thinking hemlock might work and he was going to research it."

There's a beat of silence as he looks at me.

"I'm so sorry." I want to reach out and hug him but I don't know if he'll want me to—not after I've bombarded him with some pretty shitty secrets.

"My dad was thinking about murdering people?"

I nod and he shakes his head.

"No, that's not possible. Dad would never do something like that. Ever. Are you sure you heard it right?"

"Yes. I heard it, clear as I can hear you talking now."

He gets up from the bed and starts pacing the floor, a frown on his face. I watch him, trying to keep as quiet as possible—to give him time to think but also trying not to remind him I was the one who just wrecked the image of his dad.

Eventually, he stops and grabs his shirt from out of the cupboard.

"Come on," he says, pulling it over his head.

"Where are we going?"

"To talk to my dad."

Chapter 5

Oliver's quiet in the car. And he doesn't look at me, which makes me feel like a really bad person for ever having said something. Makes me wish, not for the first time and probably not the last, that I didn't have this stupid, crappy, creepy power.

But there's no going back now. At least he hasn't run screaming out of my life.

Yet.

I chew my fingernail, ripping it from its safe place in my nail bed. Oliver reaches over and takes my hand, holding it in his.

"Stop. I'm not blaming you for any of this. I'm just going to talk to him... work out what's happening."

I wrap my fingers around his.

"How can you be so understanding about this?" My voice is soft in the confines of the car. "I mean, I'm glad you are but I think I'd be freaking out and ... I don't know, blaming me or something."

He glances at me. "I don't blame you. It's not your fault my dad... well, that he had those thoughts. Although I'm sure there's a logical explanation. And if I'm truthful, I *am* a bit freaked out. But I love you, so I'll get past it. It's as simple as that."

I blink hard, trying to stop the tears welling in my eyes from making their way to my cheeks. "You know, if we were at home and not going to confront your dad about having murderous thoughts, you'd so be getting lucky now."

He laughs but there's no more talking the rest of the way. The house is dark when we pull up but then, it is almost midnight.

"Do you think they'll be in bed?"

He turns off the car. "Mum will be, but Dad's a night owl. It doesn't get to sleep until one, usually."

"Do you want me to stay in the car?" I want him to say yes with every fibre of my being. Another mark to me being a coward and honestly, I'm okay with that.

"No," he says, pausing before opening the door. "I'd like it if you'd come in with me. And I'd like to tell Dad what you can do but only if you're okay with it."

All thoughts in my brain freeze for a second.

"You want to tell him?" The words squeak out of my mouth, strangled by the tightness of my throat.

He swivels in his seat. "I know I'm asking a lot but if he doesn't know what you can do, how am I going to confront him about this thought?"

When he says it like that, it makes perfect sense. But I still don't want anyone else to know. People treat me differently once they know—my mother, my best friend at school. And Oliver's parents like me. What if they make it so horrible he breaks up with me? What if they see me as a total freak and don't want me anywhere around? People go weird when they realize I know what they're thinking—when I know their secrets.

It must show on my face how much I hate the idea, because he takes my hand again.

"It'll be okay. I promise."

I want to believe him but I can't think—the panic is pulling my thoughts apart.

"Please."

The look on his face does it. I nod. Just once. "Okay. But only your dad. No one else."

"Deal. Only Dad."

The walk up to their front door feels like I'm marching to the gallows. Oliver stops and kisses me—a fortifying one—before texting his dad to tell him we're at the front door.

It's only a minute before it's answered and Michael is standing there in his pyjamas, smile on his face.

"Well, hello, you two. To what do I owe the honour of a visit at this time of night? Everything okay?"

"Yeah, we just needed to have a quick chat," Oliver says, giving his dad a hug as we go in. "Mum asleep?"

"Yes, it's been a big day and she was up early this morning helping Sarah get ready. Do you want me to wake her?"

"No, no. It's all good. We wanted to chat to you."

Michael frowns. "Well, that sounds serious. Do you want to come into my study?"

Oliver nods and I follow them down a hallway with a glossy wooden floor, passing rooms that look like they're from a showroom. Somehow, I can't see Oliver in this house but maybe I'm just used to his.

The study is the stereotypical one you see in movies. Bookshelves line two of the walls, and there is a solid, wooden desk with a leather chair behind it. We sit on a brown leather couch while Michael leans against his desk.

"Okay, what's going on?" *Oh shit, what if they're pregnant? She seems nice but they've only started going out.*

Oliver leans forward and takes a deep breath.

"Dad, Bree has... well, she had a special talent."

"Right." He gives me a quick smile, but I can see the confusion on his face.

"And I need you to keep an open mind."

"Open mind. Gotcha."

"Okay." He takes another breath and I want to sink into the couch—disappear from view. "Bree can hear thoughts. She's a telepath."

Michael does the combination frown and smile again. "What?"

It's my turn—I need to back Oliver up. "I can hear people's thoughts. Everyone's thoughts."

"Well." He shakes his head. "Well, that's not what I expected to hear. And you'll have to forgive me, but it's a bit hard to believe. Is this a joke? Getting one over your old man?"

Oliver shakes his head. "No Dad–"

"You were wondering if we were pregnant. Before, just as we sat down. You thought it and hoped we weren't because we hadn't been together long."

Michael's mouth hangs open as he looks at me. And then, as if he realizes what he's doing, he snaps it shut.

"What's going on here?"

"Dad, when we were at the wedding, Bree heard your thoughts. She didn't mean to; it's not something she can stop. And, for some reason, she can't hear all of them—yours and mine — just some."

Michael glances at me again, and I nod.

"And so, when we were at the wedding, she heard some of your thoughts and..." He looks at me. "Well, she heard you planning to kill someone. She heard you planning a murder, Dad."

Michael's eyes go wide as he glances between us. And then he does something so unexpected it's my turn to be confused.

He laughs. Big belly laughs that make him fall slightly sideways on the desk, leaning against his hand; laughter that keeps going until he's crying and even then, he's still laughing. I wonder, for a second, if the reason he was thinking about murder is that he's having a breakdown and, by coming here, we've caused the final break.

Eventually, he stops and sits back up, sucking in big breaths.

"Are you okay?" Oliver looks like he's just as confused.

"Yes," Michael says. "I'm good. Thank you for coming here. For checking with me first."

"So, is it true? Did you have those thoughts?"

Michael smiles. "It's true. I was thinking about how to murder someone. A couple of people actually. I think I've settled on the idea of poisoning them."

"Dad, Jesus! I can't believe–"

Oliver's shock is just as great as mine. I mean, I know I heard it but I expected he'd at least try to deny it! Oliver lurches forward in his seat but his dad holds up his hand to stop him.

"There's a good reason for it," he says, moving around behind the desk. "Let me show you something."

"God, Dad, how can you say that? There's never a good reason for murdering someone!"

But his dad smiles again and brings out what looks like a whole ream of paper.

"Looks like it's a night for sharing secrets," he says,

winking at me and handing us the paper. "You're both the first to know."

I look down. Black letters are stark on the white page:

Booked for Murder
A novel
By Michael Smit

"You're writing a book?" I shake my head.

"I am," says Michael. "And I'd love to hear more about you being a telepath. It sounds fascinating."

It's going to be hard to say no after what I've accused him of. And maybe, just maybe, that'll be okay...

Third Time Lucky

Erin grinned as she passed me a glass of champagne.

'This is a hell of an art opening, Kat.'

I sighed out a deep, shuddering breath, trying to let go of the anxiety that filled every cell of my body. Even though the gallery was full. Full! All these people, here to see my paintings. I shook my head.

'I still can't believe it.'

'Well, you should. Haven't I been telling you for years that you need to have a show? Your paintings are amazing.'

'Yeah, but as my best friend, you're biased.'

She moved her glass towards mine. 'Here's to best friends being right then.'

I clinked my glass on hers and she took a step back, a scandalized expression on her face. 'What are you doing?'

'What?' I looked at my glass, trying to work out what was wrong.

'Oh my God, sometimes I can't believe we're even friends! How can you make a toast without looking me in the eyes? Don't you know that means seven years bad sex?'

I laughed. 'You've got to be having sex for it to be bad.'

She scrunched her nose up at me. 'Well, just because you're in a drought doesn't mean all of us are and it's not worth taking the risk.'

I sighed. She was right. I was in a drought. A long, hot, drawn-out drought that wasn't promising rain anytime soon, even though I would've been happy to get saturated. I missed being in a relationship. I missed sleeping in with someone and Sunday breakfasts and cuddles and watching movies and laughing. And I missed the sex. Well, the good sex. Definitely not the bad. But with trying to get ready for the exhibition and building my name as an artist, there didn't seem to be any guys willing to take a back seat when I needed them to. Actually, for ages, there hadn't been a guy I'd wanted anywhere near the car, let alone in a seat.

I touched the necklace that was my talisman, feeling the smooth warmth of the amethyst under my fingers. Erin looked at me and snorted before taking another sip of her champagne.

'What?' I said, dropping the necklace.

'You'd be fine if you weren't still hung up on Lucas.'

'I'm not hung up on him.' But I didn't like the way my voice went up at the end, like even my brain didn't quite believe me.

'Yeah, sure. Whatever you say.'

'I'm not! That was a long time ago.' Six years and seven months, to be exact.

'Isn't that the necklace he gave you?'

'Yes, but that doesn't mean anything. I just like it.'

She snorted again. I took a sip of champagne, trying to ignore her, focusing on the cool, sweet bubbles on my tongue instead. Although maybe she had a point. A small one. The tiniest sliver. Not that I'd admit that to her.

I remembered the night when Lucas had given me the amethyst. Our first Christmas together. He'd secured it around my neck, his fingers warm on my skin, telling me it was to help with creativity, focus and belief in myself. Telling me he thought I was a great painter and I should share it with the world. Convincing me that maybe...just maybe... I could. And then wrapping me in a hug, kissing me until all I could think about was him.

It didn't mean I was still hung up on him though, did it? Just because I still wore it? I'd had other relationships since he'd left to be a part of Doctors without Borders, feeling like he needed to do more. Be more. Not wanting to end our three-year relationship but not settled either. So, I'd let him go without reproach or guilt. Because I loved him. Even if I cried for nine months and didn't paint for almost a year. Even if it took Erin getting angry with me to pull me out of it.

And my other relationships since then had been...fine. Nice. Not Lucas but nice. Just not nice enough to keep going.

I sighed and gave Erin a half smile. 'I'm not still hung up on him. He's gone. We're on different continents. But he was an important part of all this.' I gestured with my glass to the paintings hanging on the wall.

'I know. But now you're here—a huge success if the number of 'sold' red dots being put on the walls are any indication. You should have someone to celebrate with. Someone special. You deserve it.'

'I do. I have you.' I smiled at her and she grinned back at me.

'Yes, but I've been eying off the guy over there all night. And I think he might be my reward for your success.'

Laughing, I clinked glasses with her again. 'Well then, far be it from me to deny you your reward.'

She gave me a fierce hug, full of love and friendship. 'You're the best friend ever. I'm so goddam proud of you.'

'Thank you. For everything.'

She stood back, glaring at me. 'Don't you dare make me cry. I'm off to be irresistibly flirty. I can't do that with red eyes.'

'Oh, just go.' I laughed again and watched as she went over to make her move on the guy she'd pointed out.

Sometimes, just sometimes, I was jealous of her confidence with men. I knew I was okay looking. Hazel eyes in a face that was pleasant but not striking, blond hair that was probably my one vanity and a curvy body, which Lucas had always told me he loved. Lucas. It seemed to all come back to him tonight. I wasn't sure why.

I glanced around the room, taking in the number of people who'd come. Some of them, I knew, were just here for the free food and wine, but there were others who liked what I did. Others who thought I was a real artist, even if I still doubted it myself sometimes. I reached up to touch the amethyst again. Self-belief. I definitely needed that tonight.

People were still wandering in, even though the exhibition was more than halfway through, and I watched them taking in my paintings. And then stopped; frozen for a moment. I'd have known that body anywhere, the shape of him, the way he moved, the way he pushed his hand through his hair as he looked around. Lucas. As if my thoughts had pulled him into existence. Stupid.

He turned, his eyes finding mine, and my breath caught. Cliched, but there you go. He made me lose my breath. Only him. Maybe Erin was right.

This wasn't the first time I'd seen him since we'd broken

up. Unexpectedly, three years ago, he'd been at a mutual friend's Christmas party. It'd been hard. Harder than I would've thought after that long apart. He'd wrapped me in a hug, the smell of him overwhelming me, taking me right back to when we'd been together and everything had been... right. The low cough from my boyfriend at the time, Steven, had brought both of us back to reality. Poor Steven. He'd had to put up with the three of us talking all night. Well, Lucas and I, talking, chatting, remembering, and him being the third wheel. We'd broken up soon after but, by that time, Lucas had gone back overseas. And I was heartbroken all over again.

And now, here he was, after another three years.

I watched him as he walked towards me. He was leaner than when I'd seen him last but looked stronger—the muscles in his arms evident in the white button-up shirt he wore. His face was more sculptured too—his cheekbones and jaw line sharp, like the last few years had been hard. And his dark hair was longer than he used to wear it, enough that it touched the collar of his shirt. He carried himself like a man with a purpose and control. I wondered what'd happened to have changed him from the young, carefree man I'd known.

He smiled at me as he came closer and I saw him then—the Lucas I remembered. The Lucas I'd loved. Even if there were a few more crinkles around his green eyes, this was his smile. The shock of seeing him made me almost forget to smile back and then he was there, taking my hands, engulfing them in his.

'Kat.' His voice—the way he said my name—made everything lower than my chest feel like it was melting away.

'Lucas. I can't believe you're here!'

He smiled again. 'I had to come and see the exhibition of my favourite artist.'

His thumb rubbed over the top of my hands, distracting me, my brain struggling to focus on his words when his touch made my skin tingle.

'I didn't even know you were back. You should've let me know.'

'I've only been back for...' he turned our hands slightly to check his watch, 'four hours. So, consider yourself told.'

'You must be tired!' Maybe that was the reason for shadows under his eyes. 'You didn't have to come.'

But I was glad he had.

'I wanted to.' He looked around, like he was searching for something, and I raised an eyebrow at him in question. 'I'm just checking that there's no boyfriend hanging around to punch me if I hug you.'

I felt the blush creep up my neck to my cheeks. 'No, no boyfriend.'

His smile got bigger. 'Well then.'

And he pulled me towards him, wrapping his arms around me. God, I'd forgotten how good it felt. The smell of him, clean and earthy; sandalwood and him. I closed my eyes, allowing myself to enjoy the feel of him, just for a moment. The feel of his arms around me, the hardness of his chest against my cheek, the solidness of him.

'I'm so proud of you,' he murmured.

I took a deep breath—a final moment—before I pulled back out of his embrace. Because I couldn't put myself through this again. Seeing him, touching him, wanting him, only for him to leave once more. I needed to be strong.

I put on a smile that felt too bright.

'Well, I'm glad you're here. Do you want to see some of my canvases?'

I could see the confusion in his eyes for a second, so quickly come and gone that I wondered if I'd imagined it. He nodded.

'Sure. That's why I'm here, after all.'

I was careful not to touch him as we walked around the gallery, even though I was aware of his hand next to mine, the closeness of his body as he leant in to listen when I answered his questions about the paintings, the heat in his gaze as he looked at me.

We were halfway around the room when Erin came over. She didn't look happy but then, maybe that was something only I noticed as her best friend.

'Lucas! Wow, I didn't know you were back. And that you were coming tonight.'

Lucas looked at me and then back at Erin, a guarded look in his eyes. Maybe I wasn't the only one to notice...

'Nice to see you again, Erin. No, I didn't know I'd be here either. But I saw a story about the exhibition in the magazine on the plane and knew I had to get here.'

'Did you? That's lucky.'

Her lips tightened, and I knew she was about to grill him. Not because she was horrible, just protective. And I didn't want that. I didn't want to hear how long he was back for this time or if he was involved with someone. I wanted to get through the night with no expectations or hope. It was nice he'd come. That was all.

It was perfect timing then, when Sandra, the gallery owner, came over to us.

'Kat, I think it's time for a speech.'

She warned me I'd have to make one, even though the thought of public speaking had my heart going at triple its normal beat and I wasn't sure if I'd get any moisture back in my suddenly dry mouth. I clutched at my necklace without even thinking, Lucas's eyes drawn to the movement, and I saw a small smile at the corners of his mouth before I dropped it again. I didn't need to be sending mixed messages. Be strong. Friends! That was it!

I nodded to Sandra. 'Okay. Where would you like me?'

I followed her on shaking legs and looked down at my notes already assembled on the lectern. My speech was short and to the point. People were here for my art, not for me. I cleared my throat and adjusted the microphone before clearing my throat again and rubbing my sweaty palms down my pants. God. I hated this. I looked up. Everyone was watching me but all I could see was Lucas and Erin towards the back of the crowd. Erin was glaring at Lucas, her finger pointing at him. Level three on the anger charts then. Lucas looked unaffected, even though he couldn't be. Not in the face of the fox terrier that Erin could become.

I needed to get this over and done with as quickly as possible and try to save him from whatever Erin felt she needed to lecture him about. I wasn't letting my heart go there but he was still my friend. That fact made the speech easier than it normally would've been and soon, it was over. People were clapping politely before Sandra took over and told everyone that twenty-four of the thirty-two paintings had already been sold. Twenty-four!

I smiled, hurriedly moving away from the front of the crowd, needing to be out of the public eye. Lucas smiled at me and rubbed his hand up my arm—the feel of his hand on my skin making everything in me tighten. Everything. I wanted him. There. I'd acknowledged it. But it wasn't going to happen. I was being firm.

'You did well,' he said. 'And congratulations on the sales. Looks like I got here too late. I might need you to do one on commission for me.'

God, oh god. I would give him anything. No. No! Big breath. I could do this.

'Yes, you did really well,' said Erin, smiling at me before turning to shoot Lucas a look that promised certain death if he wasn't careful. 'Well, I'll... leave you to it.'

I frowned at her retreating back.

'What was that about?'

Lucas raised his eyebrows. 'What?'

I turned my frown on him. 'What were you guys talking about during the speech?'

He tried to maintain a look of innocence but it only took a moment of silence before he sighed.

'She was warning me not to hurt you again. Told me in no uncertain terms that if I did, she'd hurt me.'

I felt everything in me stop. Every organ, every thought —all of it, stopped, just for a second, before it all started again at super speed.

I licked my lips. 'And what did you say?'

He took my hand, his eyes looking at the ring I had on, twisting it like it was the most fascinating thing in the world, until I was about to scream. Finally, he looked up at me.

'I told her I didn't want to hurt you. I never wanted to hurt you.'

'Oh.' Not particularly eloquent but I didn't know what else to say.

He reached up to touch my cheek and I had to steal myself not to lean into his hand.

'I'm sorry if I hurt you before.'

I looked away from the intensity in his eyes, not wanting to see the longing in there. Or to wish I was seeing it, maybe.

I shrugged, trying to smile. 'It was a long time ago. And we've moved on. It is what it is.'

He smiled too but it didn't look like a real one any more than mine did.

'Yes, it was a long time ago.' He gestured to the necklace. 'I'm glad you still wear it.'

I touched it. 'It's my talisman.'

He nodded, silent again.

'So,' I said, trying to keep my voice cheery, 'how long are you back for this time?'

He leant against the wall, watching me.

'I'm back for good.'

My heart tripped over itself and I tried to calm it with a deep breath.

'Oh. You aren't going back overseas?'

He shook his head. 'I've got a job at the hospital.'

'Oh.'

That's was all I could say—again! I swear I knew my words. And yet, the only thing my brain seemed to be able to concentrate on was that he was back. For good. For good! He. Was. Back.

'I missed you,' he said. 'All the time. Every day.'

'Did you?' My heart stepped up another notch, hopeful, even though I'd told it not to be. He touched my hand again, threading his fingers through mine, and I let him. Traitorous brain.

'Yes. You know, I've been thinking. We were together three years, and then apart for three, and then three more. Do you think...?'

I watched him, waiting, not wanting to make myself vulnerable by talking first. Unfair, I know.

He took a deep breath. 'Do you think you might want to try again? With us? Third time lucky?'

Yes. Yes, yes, yes. But could I? Was I brave enough?

He leant closer to me, his green eyes full of promise. And I knew I was. I had to be. Because I wanted him.

'Yes,' I said.

'Yes?'

I nodded. 'Yes.'

He kissed me then, his lips soft against mine, his hand on my back, pulling me closer, and I thought that maybe three was my new lucky number.

Bad Guy

Chapter 1

Her biscuits could definitely become my kryptonite.

They're perfect—not too chewy, not too crunchy and with just the right ratio of choc chips. Best. Ever.

Although to be fair, I've ever actually tasted home-made cookies before. Not that I can remember, anyway. Maybe my mum made us some before she died, but I doubt it.

How sad is that? Seventeen years old and I've never had a home-made biscuit. Seventeen today, in fact. Happy frigging birthday to me...

Mrs Bailey sets another plate of biscuits in front of me, beside the cup of milk she's already poured. She's the image of a perfect, loving grandmother—light, grey hair, wrinkles that look like they've come from a lifetime of smiling... she's even wearing an apron, for Christ's sake. Just a shame she's not my grandmother.

'You've done such a good job at mowing the lawn, and all that weeding you did... are you sure thirty dollars is enough?'

'More than enough,' I say, smiling at her. 'I only did the front.'

'And you don't know how grateful I am for that. I still love gardening but I don't have the stamina to push the mower anymore and ever since Frank died...' Her voice falls away.

'Was he your husband?' I try to keep my voice soft; respectful. Even though this is the information I'm actually here for. Which makes me feel like a total jerk.

'Yes,' she smiles at me. It's a sad one. 'He died two years ago. We'd been married sixty-two years.'

'Wow, that's a long time.' The awe in my voice isn't pretend. Not this time, anyway. Although I pretend to be someone else so often it's hard to say what my real emotions are anymore. Except for how I feel about Jimmy. My twin's the only *real* thing in my whole, frigging sad life.

Mrs Bailey chuckles. 'Yes, I suppose it must feel like that to someone as young as you. It feels like an amazingly short time, however. And the last two years seemed to have lasted forever.'

I look over to the cabinet filled with old things—the reason I'm here. 'Was he interested in antiques?'

She sits down in the chair beside me and nods. 'Yes. Frank was a bit of an amateur historian. He loved anything with a history to tell. The bedroom at the back of the house is filled with more of his finds. I just can't bring myself to give them away.'

My heart pounds at the possibility that the knife—the one Gep, my step-father, wants us to steal — might be here. It's the best lead I've had so far, anyway.

'Yeah, I can understand his fascination. I love old things.'

I don't. I hate them. Probably because that's all Gep

makes us steal. And they're the things that help him increase his power—that make him more of a sadistic bastard than he already is. But to keep Jimmy safe, I'm willing to do almost anything.

And getting the knife will keep Jimmy safe.

She smiles at me. A big one that makes the wrinkles in her face crease and fills her face with joy. 'Oh Penn, you don't know how happy it makes me to hear that. I find so many of the young ones now a days aren't interested in learning about our history. When you come back tomorrow to do the rest of the yard, would you like to have a look at his collection? I can get some of the more interesting pieces out tonight?'

I do a mental fist pump and try to look excited but not too excited—keeping the enthusiasm just right. 'That'd be great.'

She nods. 'Well then, young man, it's a date.'

She gets up and I stand with her, glancing at the rest of the biscuits on the plate out of the corner of my eye. Damn, they were good. I don't know if she sees the look or if she's just a genuinely nice person—the last one, I think—but she picks up the plate and moves towards the kitchen.

'Let me put these in a container and you can take them home.'

'You don't have to,' I say, even as my brain's telling me to shut the hell up. She ignores me anyway, pressing the plastic container into my hands.

'Nonsense. It's nice to have someone who enjoys them so much. And do you have brothers or sisters you could share them with?'

'Yeah, my twin brother, Jimmy. And my two younger brothers.'

'Oh, a twin!' she says, clutching her hands in front of her like I've made her day—her week. 'I knew I liked you.'

'Are you a twin yourself?'

She nods, but the joy goes from a face a bit, like a balloon leaking helium. 'Yes. I am. Or I was. She died a long time ago, when we were twenty-one.'

I swallow hard. The thought of losing Jimmy has my stomach twisting, screwing up on itself like my whole body is rebelling at the idea.

'I'm sorry.' My voice is soft. And I really am. I can't imagine what that'd be like.

She touches my arm and gives me a half smile. 'It was a long time ago. But I still miss her. Every day. Make sure you look after each other.'

I nod, wanting to tell her that's all I do. It's the reason I'm here, at this house, ready to rob her, even though she's a nice lady and doesn't deserve it. Even though it's a shitty thing to do. To keep Jimmy safe, I'll be the bad guy.

Chapter 2

The house Gep found for us in this town is an old, low set brick house. Nothing special. Nothing that stands out. Typical of what he usually tries to rent. The less we stand out, the easier it is to steal what we need and get out of town without too many people noticing.

I stand looking at the front door, it's blue paint fading and peeling. Feels like a bit of a metaphor for our life, really. Shitty and second rate. I shake my head, angry at the self-pity. Jesus, suck it up.

One more year. That's all I need to get through. Just one more year and then Jimmy and I can take off—get the hell away from Gep and his sadistic bullshit. Taking a deep breath in, I square my shoulders before turning the handle and pushing the door open.

I walk into an empty lounge but that doesn't surprise me. It'd have to be the most depressing room we've ever had in all the houses we've lived in. Although we've lived in so many, it's hard to be sure. The brown and yellow pile carpet and the avocado green paint on the walls don't make you want to linger. And it's the hottest room in the house. Just for once, I'd like to live in a place that's halfway decent. But then, there's so many things I wish for, it's actually really far down the list.

Gep is sitting at the table at the back of the house, newspaper spread in front of him. Our step-father. Although that term's only ever loosely applied to him because he's definitely not father material. Guardian, maybe. Jailer... that's probably more accurate.

He looks up when I come in. 'Did you find it?'

No greeting, which I want to make a sarcastic comment about, the words sitting on the tip of my tongue, waiting to spew out of my mouth, but I'm not that stupid. Not at the moment, anyway. I go to the fridge instead, giving myself a minute as I open the door.

'I haven't actually seen it yet, but I'm sure it's there. I'm going back tomorrow. She's going to show me some stuff then.'

I catch his nod out of the corner of my eye. 'Good. Then we should be able to go by mid-week.'

Mid-week. Jesus, we haven't even been in this town three weeks yet. I've only just finished my assignment for English. How the hell am I ever going to pass school and get a job that supports Jimmy and me when we leave here? Just another thing to hate Gep for... as if I need any more reasons.

'I don't know that I'll be able to get it by then. Only if she shows it to me tomorrow. Otherwise, it might take longer.' I turn to watch his reaction, survival instinct kicking in.

His eyes narrow but he stays in his seat. 'Mid-week, Penn.'

I can feel the anger growing in me, like a chemical

reaction in my gut, rising from my stomach to my chest, making me stupid. That's the only reason I say what I do.

'Christ, she's a nice lady. And it's her husband's stuff and she still loves him, even though he's dead. If I take the knife, it'll... I don't know... it'll make her sad. It's wrong.'

He stands this time and I take a step back as he walks towards me, even though I shouldn't because it just makes me look weak. But I can't help it. I know what's coming, and curse the stupid part of my brain that makes me open my mouth.

'She's a *nice* lady?' He sneers at me. 'Oh, why then, by all means, let's just skip this one.' He's right in my face now and I can feel the heat from his body. I tense, waiting for his reaction. 'I'm doing this for you. For all you boys. Protecting you, you little shit.'

I snort. Stupid. Moronic. But it slips out before I can help it.

His hand comes up, ready to touch me, and I shut my eyes, waiting for it, adrenalin screaming through my system, telling me to run. Run. Just get away.

But the burn—the way he tortures us to keep us in line—doesn't come. He just laughs at me instead, which makes me feel worse. Because he knows I'm weak. He knows he has power over me. And that screws with my brain more than the pain.

He takes a step back, and I open my eyes. The sadistic grin on his face makes me want to shut them again.

'Pathetic. Just steal the fucking knife, Penn. Like a good boy.'

He walks out of the room and it's only then I take a shuddering breath, putting a hand up to my chest to ease the pain of a heart that doesn't understand what the hell's going on. I slam the fridge shut and lean against it, trying to stop the threatening tears. He's right, I am pathetic. If I could've taken Jimmy with me, I would've left years ago.

As if my thoughts call him into existence, I hear the sound of wheelchair tyres on the floor. I don't look up straight away, not wanting my brother to see my moment of self-frigging-pity, even though I know he'd understand.

'Are you okay?' he says, the words not coming cleanly out of his mouth. A brain injury when he was three from the same car accident that killed our mum left him like this. Not that it makes any difference—he's my brother, that's all that matters.

I turn around and give him and Fox, who's pushing his chair, a smile I know isn't fooling anyone.

'Yeah, all good. Just Gep...'

'Being a psycho,' he says, finishing my sentence, and all I can do is nod.

I grab the container of biscuits I put on top of the fridge when I came in, and hold them out. 'Biscuits for you guys if you want them. Home-made.'

Fox grabs them, opening the lid and taking a huge sniff. I can't stop the real grin that comes to my face this time as I watch him and he grins back at me — a rare sight. There aren't usually a lot of smiles in this family.

He pushes Jimmy to the table and we sit, the biscuits in front of them, like neither of them are game enough to touch them. Fox pushes his hand through his shockingly red hair and looks at me.

'Are these from the old lady you think's got the knife?'

'Yeah.' I nod, and then sigh. 'They're really good.'

'What's the sigh for?' Jimmy asks, taking his eyes off the biscuits for a moment to look at me.

I shrug. 'She's nice, you know? Misses her husband. I'm

pretty sure the knife, if it's there, will be his. And I just feel...bad.'

Fox lips go into a thin line. 'It's not the first time we've taken something from someone nice. Or who doesn't deserve to be robbed. Stop overthinking it.'

I know these words coming out of his mouth by heart–I say them to myself all the time. But still... I hate this. Hate what Gep makes us do. Hate what he forces us to be. It's not a life. It's just shit.

I take a biscuit from the container and break it, giving half to Jimmy. He holds it in his hand, looking at it for a moment before looking back up, his eyes serious.

'Don't take it, then. If it makes you feel bad, just don't take it.'

I grimace and Fox sits back hard in his seat, muttering a soft 'shit'. Jimmy, the good one out of the lot of us. The one who gives a damn about other people.

'I have to. You know what Gep will be like if I don't.'

Jimmy's face screws up in concern but he's saved from having to answer when Kat comes in and slumps onto one of the chairs. He's the youngest of the four of us, probably the most optimistic too. But then, he's only had twelve years of Gep's crap, so maybe it hasn't worn him down yet. Not that Jimmy and I are related to him or Fox—I'm not even sure if Gep is their dad; he just came home with them as babies...first Fox and then Kat and I'd learnt a long time ago it was better not to ask questions, but they're close enough to brothers that we call ourselves that, especially when we start a new school so regularly.

'What's wrong with you?' Fox says, watching Kat chew on his bottom lip.

Kat slumps even lower. 'Gep just said we might be moving by the middle of the week. He said you'd found the knife.' He shoots me a look that's half accusing, even though he knows the deal—as soon as we steal something, Gep moves us on.

'Maybe. I'm not sure yet. I haven't actually seen it.'

He sits up at that, the start of a smile on his face. He can go from sad to hopeful so fast it gives me whiplash sometimes and then I feel bad that maybe I've given him false hope.

'I'm pretty sure it's there though,' I say quickly, not wanting to make him feel like crap, just... keeping him grounded in reality. Which sounds shitty, even in my own head.

He leans forward and grabs one of the biscuits out of the container, shoving half of it in his mouth. 'Wow, these are really good!' He waves the other half around as he talks through the mouthful of crumbs. 'But you haven't seen it yet so it might not be there and then we won't have to move and I can stay here and go to the party at Zac's house next week. It's a pool party—I've never been to a pool party. Do you think, even if you find it, Gep will be okay if you steal it next week? Then I can still go.'

'Not a chance,' Fox says, and I'm torn between being glad that I'm not the only grinch squashing Kat's dreams and feeling crappy that the poor kid can't just go to a pool party like any other kid. All we want is a normal life. It doesn't have to even be exciting. Just... real.

'Yeah, but Penn might not find it. Isn't that right, Penn?' The hope in his eyes wears me down and I nod.

'Sure, Kat. Maybe.'

Of course, that's when Gep comes back into the room. It's like he's got a bullshit radar. His eyes narrow and he looks at all of us before they land on the container of biscuits.

'What the fuck are they?' His voice is harsh, cutting across the silence as we watch him...watch and wait to see what shit he's going to pull.

I dig my fingers into my thighs. 'They're biscuits. From the lady I think has the knife.'

He laughs, but it's not a nice one. It's one that has my whole body on alert and I can see all the others look just as tense.

'Well, isn't that so frigging sweet? Biscuits for the boys! Almost makes you not want to rob her, doesn't it?'

I know better than to answer that.

He leans down slowly, placing his hands on the table in between Kat and Fox. Neither of them looks at him, even though he makes a point of staring at all of us in turn. And then, without warning, he sweeps his hand across the table, sending the container smashing into the wall, biscuits pieces spraying over the floor.

'There'll be no staying past mid-week. Penn will find the knife tomorrow, take it and we'll be leaving.'

I see the emotion flit over Fox's face and want to tell him to just shut up, but he's a big boy—only a few years younger than Jimmy and me, and he knows what Gep's like. Still, my gut twists itself in knots as his mouth opens.

'What if it's not there? The knife. Penn said he hasn't seen it yet. Then we'd have to stay longer and Kat could go to the party.'

Gep stands back up, and it feels even more threatening than when he was leaning over.

'The knife will be there. And there'll be no god damn party.'

'Kat just wants to go to the party—'

But he doesn't get to finish. Because that's when Gep

touches his arm and Fox's body goes stiff, the pain clear on his face.

The burn.

Gep's own personal torture. I don't know how he does it —some shit magical power thing—but I know an electrical current is pouring through Fox's body right now, paralysing him, making him sit there and just take it. And none of us do anything about it, because it could just as easily be one of us copping it. And even though it's a crap way to think, the only thing I care about is that Gep's not doing it to Jimmy.

It doesn't matter how nice Mrs Bailey is; I know I need to get that knife. There's no other option.

Chapter 3

I hesitate before I knock on her door the next morning. But then, I see Fox's face in my mind again and know next time, Gep will target Jimmy, like he's done before. Just to keep me in line. It's how he controls me, even when he goes on and on about family and protecting us— protecting us from the spirits *he* frigging calls up. That's why he wants all this stuff, so he can have more control over the spirits he gets his energy from. God, my life is all kinds of messed up.

I step forward and knock.

Mrs Bailey smiles at me when she answers it and that makes me feel even worse.

'Penn, it's so lovely to see you again. How did your brothers enjoy the biscuits?'

I hold up the container and smile at her, playing the part even though I don't feel it. Playing at being someone else—whoever I need to be in that moment to get the information I need. I've done it so long now I'm not even sure who the real Penn is anymore, except when I'm around Jimmy.

'They loved them,' I say. 'They said to say thanks.'

'Oh, isn't that sweet,' she says, beaming at me. 'Well, come on inside then and I'll show you Frank's collection. I've been sorting through it all night, getting out some of the things I thought you might be interested in.'

'Umm, do you want me to do the mowing first?'

She laughs. 'Oh, of course. I almost forgot you were here to finish the lawn, I was so excited to show you Frank's things. You do that and then come on in. I'll have a cold drink and some cookies waiting for you.'

I smile at her again and head to the shed to drag out the mower. For the next hour, as I push it around the yard, all I can think about is whether I can do this. Whether I still *want* to do this. Not that I've ever wanted to, but still... And all I keep coming back to is that it'll protect Jimmy. Even if it hurts other people.

I clean off the mower and put it away, organising things in the shed so it makes it easier for her. Putting off going inside. Pathetic. I sigh and walk over to the house, knocking on the door again.

'Come in, dear,' Mrs Bailey calls out and I open the door and go in, feeling awkward as I take the opportunity to look around. No knife. Not that I can see in that quick glance anyway.

'I'm in the dining room,' she calls and I follow her voice into the same room I was in yesterday. She has a plate of biscuits on the table and what looks like iced tea in a glass next to it. And spread over the rest of the space is what I can only assume are parts of her husband's collection.

She beams at me. 'Come and sit. You can eat while I show you some of the things.'

I smile back and pull up a chair at the table, my eyes tracking over the items. And there, on the other side to me, is the knife Gep wants. Silver Damascus blade, with an intricate carving in the black handle, filled in with mother-of-pearl. It has to be it. There can't be two blades like it in this town. And the spirit Gep called up told him it was here. That's why we came to this backwater in the first place.

'Wow,' I say, trying to not make it obvious that I'm looking at the knife, because if I call attention to it, she'll definitely know it's me when I take it. 'You husband had a lot of cool stuff.'

'Yes,' she said. 'I had a man from the museum come last year and he told me it's all quite valuable and I could get some good money for it from a collector. But I told him I'd never sell any of it. This was Frank's pride and joy. It's not about the money.'

I smile at her, feeling my chest tighten, knowing I'm going to break her heart. 'You must've really loved him?'

Her eyes get suspiciously damp and I shift in my seat, not knowing how to react if she starts crying. She smiles at me though, even if it is a bit wobbly. 'He was my soul mate. I knew it as soon as I met him when we were eighteen. And then he helped me get through the loss of my Jeannie — my twin. I don't know if I would've ever managed to start living again without him.'

I don't know what to say to that and she must see how uncomfortable I am because she pats my hand and gives a small laugh.

'Anyway, you don't want to hear about all of that soppy stuff. Let me show you what he collected.'

For the next twenty minutes, I honestly enjoy myself, hearing about all the cool things he had and where he got them from. Even if my eyes keep wandering back to the knife.

It's when she stands up to get more ice tea that she

insists I need after mowing the lawn for so long that it all goes to hell. Because one minute she's standing, and the next, she's collapsed on the floor, unconscious.

I race over, falling to my knees next to her, heart feeling like it's going to pound its way out of my chest. Shit. Shit, shit, shit! I don't know what to do! I touch her arm, giving it a small shake.

'Mrs Bailey.' No response. She's still breathing—I can see her chest rising and falling, so that's something. Right. An ambulance. I need to ring one. They'll know what to do. I grab my phone out of my back pocket and ring, running my hand through my blond hair, making it stick up, as I wait for them to answer.

I give them the address and sit there for what seems like forever, not knowing what to do except to grab a pillow from the lounge chair to put under her head, trying to make her more comfortable, until they get there. When they do, they take control, loading her onto a stretcher, still unconscious, and not letting me go with her when I tell them I'm not a relative.

And then I'm alone in the house. With the knife.

All I have to do is go around the table and take it. Put it in my pocket. Easiest job I've ever had to do. And yet, I don't want to. I can't. I tell myself it's just because I don't want her to be stressed when she gets home from the hospital, knowing she's been robbed. Because to think about any other reason is just way too dangerous.

Chapter 4

I don't tell Gep about seeing the knife, just that it wasn't in the stuff she showed me but that I'm going back the next afternoon to see some more. And I don't feel bad about lying—just surprised I get away with it. Usually, he senses a lie. Maybe it's the fact I wasn't lying about going back over there.

I'd rung the hospital that afternoon, heading out for a walk so Gep wouldn't overhear, and pretended to be her nephew. They told me she was expected to be back home the next day and I was taking the chance that nothing had changed.

I push Jimmy's wheelchair to the edge of the school grounds and stop, tapping my fingers on the handles.

'I'm going over to Mrs Bailey's house,' I say to the boys.

Kat's face falls. 'Did you find the knife?'

I don't know whether or not to lie. In the end, I figure the truth is better. It might hurt but at least he can prepare himself for disappointment. He should be getting used to it.

'Yeah, I saw it yesterday. But she collapsed and I had to ring for an ambulance.'

'You should have just taken it then,' Fox says, frowning at me. 'Would've been easier.'

I shrug. 'Maybe.'

'You don't want to take it,' Jimmy says, like it's a fact rather than a question. 'Don't, Penn. It doesn't matter. Let her keep it. Gep will get over it.'

I want to roll my eyes at how frigging naïve he is sometimes. Gep will *not* get over it. Gep will lose his shit and punish me by taking it out on Jimmy. And that's not happening. No matter that it makes me feel like a total arsehole to a nice old lady who's been nothing but generous.

'I going.'

Jimmy twists in his chair, looking up at me. 'It's shit, Gep forcing you to do this. You're a good person and it makes you feel bad.'

'Yeah, well, so does calling the spirits when he forces us to do it. So does never having friends outside of you guys or never having a frigging life. It's all shit.'

And I don't agree with me being a good person—if I was, I'd have told Gep to shove it long ago. But I don't say that because Jimmy will just argue with me and I'm definitely not up for it.

I take a step back and Fox moves into position behind the chair, his grey eyes serious as he looks at me. 'Will we tell Gep where you are?'

'Yeah,' I say, hoisting my bag further up my shoulder. 'Just don't tell him she collapsed, okay? Otherwise, he'll make me pay for not taking it yesterday.'

They all nod—a team, even if we've never had a choice in it. It's a matter of survival, for Fox, Jimmy and me anyway. Kat still thinks Gep could be a proper dad. And he can sometimes... on rare occasions, act caring and funny, like a real parent. And Kat's still young enough to trust in that—still has hope—while I'm always just waiting for him to change back to psycho mode. Because it never lasts. Ever.

I turn and take off at a jog, wanting to just get this over and done with. It only takes ten minutes to get there and I knock, calling out as well. The door's answered by a woman I don't know and I take a step back, suddenly feeling awkward.

'Can I help you?' she says, but she's got a smile on her face so I smile back, falling into the 'nice guy' mode that usually sucks others in—makes them feel comfortable.

'Hi, I'm Penn. I've been mowing Mrs Bailey's yard, and I was just wondering how she's going.'

'Oh.' Her smile grows wider. 'You're the young hero who rang the ambulance for her.'

I feel my face go red. Shit, a hero? I've never been called that before!

'Is she home?'

'Yes, she got home at lunchtime and I'm sure she'll want to see you. Come in, come in.' She holds the door wide open for me. 'I'm Helen, the in-home nurse. I'm just here to make sure she gets settled in and is doing okay.'

'Well, that's... great,' I say, but my mind's whirling, wondering how the hell I'm going to get the knife now. One old woman at home on her own all the time is doable. But now two people constantly here? I turn as I walk past her. 'Are you going to be able to help her out for very long?'

'I'll pop in every day and make sure she's okay, but she's pretty adamant that she doesn't need a live in nurse. And she should be fine. But it's lovely that you're worried about her. Gives me hope in our future generation.'

Which makes me feel like an even bigger shithead because all I can feel is relief that Mrs Bailey will be on her own. Jimmy was definitely wrong—I'm not a good person.

She's sitting in the lounge room when we go in, looking pale still, but better than when she collapsed yesterday. She smiles at me, holding out her hand, and I smile back as I take it in mine, thinking how...frail she seems.

'My hero,' she says and I go red again. Twice in ten minutes—Christ!

'I'm glad you're feeling better,' I say, as I sit down on the seat next to her.

'Much better,' she says. 'Thanks to you. My doctors said it was my blood pressure but they think they've got it all sorted now. If it wasn't for you though, who knows what would have happened.'

I smile at her. 'I'm just glad you're okay.' And I am. Truly.

Helen comes to the door of the lounge room. 'Alright Mrs Bailey, your medication is on the bench and your dinner is in the fridge ready for you to reheat when you're ready. I'll be back tomorrow morning around nine to check on you.' She smiles at me then. 'Are you and your family new to town?'

'Yeah.' I give her a small smile and look away, hoping it'll stop the questions.

'You're in the brick house in Kensington Street?'

I try not to react, but it's hard. How does she know that?

She smiles like she knows I'm uncomfortable. 'Don't worry, I'm not stalking you. I just live down the end of the street and thought I'd seen you and your brothers walking to school.'

'Oh, well, that's great.'

'I'm sure I'll see you again, then. See you tomorrow, Mrs Bailey. Penn.'

I just smile at her. There's no way she'll see me again

but I don't need to say that because it'll lead to questions I'm not going to answer.

'Thank you, Helen,' Mrs Bailey says and then Helen's gone, the front door clicking behind her and I'm suddenly nervous, which is stupid. Maybe it's the way Mrs Bailey's looking at me like I really am a good person. And I know I'm going to prove her wrong.

'Now,' she says, 'I want to do something as a thank you for what you did yesterday.'

'You don't have to—' I start to say, but she just waves her hand.

'Nonsense. I'm an old lady, Penn, and I get to do things because I want to do them. And I want you to pick something of Frank's. Something that you'd like to keep.'

My heart starts to triple step at her words. Shit, could it really be that easy? That I could just ask and not have to steal it?

'Are you sure?' The words are out of my mouth before my brain can tell me to shut up.

'Absolutely,' she says and her eyes look like she really means it.

'Wow. I mean, that's really generous.'

'You saved my life, Penn. It's only a small token compared to that.'

I look through to the table where everything was left yesterday and she holds her hand out towards it.

'Go and have a look. See if there's something you'd like. I know it would make Frank very happy that such a lovely young man would take care of something of his.'

And the guilt attacks again, stabbing me in the guts. I try not to let it show on my face as I get up, going over to the table and making a show of looking at everything, even though I can practically feel the knife pulling at me. I walk slowly around the other side, steady and slow, as if I don't just want to race around there and grab it.

Finally, anticipation making my movements jerky, I pick up the knife and bring it back over to her.

'What about this? Would that be okay?'

It's hard to keep my voice normal, and every nerve in my body is stretched tight as I wait for her to smile, nod her head, tell me it's perfectly fine. But she doesn't. Instead, her face drops and she looks sad—like she doesn't want to hurt me... but she's going to.

'Oh, Penn, lovely boy. Anything but that knife. I didn't even remember it was still there.'

Of course she'd say that. Of course that'd be the one thing I can't have. Because that's just how fucked up my life is. I'm so keyed up, I don't even manage to keep the disappointment from my face and she starts to tear up.

'I'm so sorry. It's only that it's my father's knife. He brought it with him from Europe after World War One and it's been in our family for generations. Frank was researching it when he died, trying to find out about its history. I just can't let you have that, Penn.'

I nod and try to smile but even the fake one – the one I always know how to do—doesn't feel comfortable on my lips. Shit. I know it's because, for just a second, I had my hopes up, like a frigging moron. Thinking that maybe, just once, I could keep Jimmy safe without having to be a thieving arse.

And now I feel even worse about having to take it from her... now I know how important it is to her. But maybe I can still get her to give it to me. Maybe if I just explain why I need it—that it's protect Jimmy. My twin. Just like she'd want to keep her twin sister safe if she was still alive... Maybe it's worth a try.

'Please, Mrs Bailey, please. Can I have the knife?'

It must be something about my tone of voice because her eyes go to my face like she's trying to find the answers in my expression.

'Please,' I say again. 'It's for my twin. To keep him safe.'

Her hand goes to her chest. 'What do you mean?'

I sit next to her again, the knife in the palm of my hand, trying to think of what I can tell her—how much truth I can put in—without telling her everything. Because 'my step-dad's a psycho who treats us like crap and does the 'burn' on us for fun. And he calls on spirits to get his powers and collects stuff like this to give him even more power' is all kinds of screwed up.

'My step-dad, he's a... collector. Of knives. And he gets... angry sometimes. Angry enough to take it out on my twin, who's got brain damage and is in a wheelchair. And I know giving my step-dad this knife would make him happy and he might be... nicer.'

Shit, even that still sounds screwed up, and I watch her face get more and more worried as the words spew out of my mouth. And I know, before she even says anything, that I've done the wrong thing. I've let someone in on our secrets and I've put Jimmy in even more danger.

I stand, like I've suddenly got somewhere important to be. 'Actually, you know what? It doesn't matter. Forget about it, it's not like that. Not really. I just thought he might like it. I'm glad you're better.'

'Penn,' she says before I move. 'Take the knife. It's yours.'

I stare at her for a moment, trying to work out if it's a trick. She stands up next to me and closes my fist around the handle.

'Please, take the knife. I don't need it anymore and if it makes you and your twin safe, then it's meant for you.'

My breathing's quick, like I've run a sprint, even though I'm just standing here.

'Are you sure?' I can't help asking the question.

'I'm sure.' She presses her lips together and I wait for her next words, even though I'm pretty sure I'm not going to like what she says. 'Is there anywhere else you can go? Someone else you and your brothers can stay with?'

I shake my head. 'No, but it's okay. It's not that bad. I was just being... dramatic. He's just strict. That's all. We're okay.'

I know I'm babbling but I need to make her believe me. I smile and try to look embarrassed, like I'm being an idiot. I don't know if the confused look on her face means I've convinced her or made it worse.

'Thank you. For the knife, I mean.'

She puts her hand over mine. 'Will you come and see me tomorrow?'

'Sure,' I say. 'Sure'.

Except I'm lying. There's no way I can come back here because that'll lead to more questions. All I'm hoping is that I haven't made things worse than they already are.

Chapter 5

I sprint home, checking behind me like I think I'm a frigging spy or something, waiting to see if someone's following me, asking questions. Which is ridiculous. Totally insane. Mrs Bailey is an old woman living on her own. There's no way she could get someone to follow me. And yet, I feel...conspicuous. Like the whole world can see me and knows the secrets I keep. Secrets for bloody Gep.

Stupid. Stupid. Stupid.

Even though I've got the knife, I can't believe I did it—told her what our life is really like; how shitty Gep actually is. Laid it all out there like there wouldn't be any consequences. It makes me want to just throw the knife away. Except that'd be even more stupid.

I slow down as I reach the house, trying to calm my panic, because Gep will know. It's like he can smell the adrenalin on me. I don't know how he does it—just as much as I'm clueless about everything he does. All I understand is he knows stuff he shouldn't, uses the things we bring him to make him stronger, calls spirits to him like he's not scared of them, fills our bodies with a painful, nerve frying, burning power that makes you want to run even though you can't move, just from touching our bare skin...

And truthfully, I don't really want to know how he does it. I just want to get Jimmy away from him.

One more year. One more year and then he can't stop us.

I hear noise coming from the back of the house when I walk in and go through. They look tense, everyone on edge, and I don't know if something's happened, or it's just everyone staying on alert around Gep.

He smiles at me when I walk in. I don't smile back. I just thrust the knife at him.

'Here. Take it.'

His grin gets wider and he takes it from me, turning it in his hands, rubbing his fingers all over it like he's trying to mark it as his own. I don't know why, but watching him makes me want to throw up. This is something Mrs Bailey treasured and now it's Geps and he's going to corrupt it like he corrupts every frigging thing that comes into his orbit.

'Does that mean we have to leave?' Kat asks, and I can hear the disappointment in his voice.

'Yes. Tomorrow. First up.' Gep grins as he looks at him. He's so absorbed in what he wants—in his power and his needs—that he doesn't even think about Kat. I don't think he even really sees him.

'Kat still wanted to go to that party this weekend,' Jimmy says, and I want to groan. Christ, I did this to keep him safe and then he goes and says something stupid.

Gep's eyes narrow. 'What?'

'Kat wanted to go to that party this weekend. And Penn didn't want to steal that knife. The lady who owned it was nice to him and he felt bad. We don't want to do this anymore.'

Jimmy's anger is embedded in every word he says and it's like it feeds my panic; that part of me that constantly needs to protect him, keep him safe, even though he never asks for it. I step forward, trying to put myself between him and Gep.

But Gep's quicker.

His hand is on Jimmy's arm before I even get a chance to stop him and I watch my brother's body go rigid under the burn I know is happening. Watch the pain wash in waves over his face. My whole body tenses, like I'm receiving it. I want to punch Gep, tackle him away from Jimmy. But I don't. I stand there, useless and pathetic, not able to protect my brother from the very person he needs the most protection from. Because I know, from previous experience, if I stop it now, it'll only make it worse. One hundred times worse.

By the time he's finished, my teeth feel like they're going to break under the force of grinding them together and my fingernails have made sharp indentations into the skin of my palms. Kat's crying silent tears that drip off his chin, watching the one person we all love being hurt, and feeling like he played a part in it. Even though he didn't. Even though all he wanted to do was to go to a frigging party—that's how screwed up Gep's made us.

Jimmy's panting, sweat pouring down his face, his body, and I go over to him, massaging the rigid muscles in his arms, trying to give him so relief.

'What the hell did you do that for?' The words are rough on my tongue like they're smart enough to want to stay in and are being forced out by the idiot who controls the brain. Me—the idiot. 'I gave you your frigging knife. Christ!'

He moves closer, pushing into my space, his power

pressing in to me and it takes all of my concentration not to take a step back. 'I did it to show that none of you get to question what I do. I make these decisions. I make them to keep you boys safe, even though none of you frigging appreciate it. It means I don't fucking care if Kat wants to go to a birthday party or if you didn't want to steal the knife because you're going to make some old bitch feel sad. You'll do what I tell you.'

A knock on the front door echoes through the house, stopping the tirade. Gep looks at Fox.

'Go and see who that is.'

Fox is only gone for a minute before he's back, his face paler than usual. He glances at me and then looks at Gep.

'It's the police. I just looked through the window.' His voice is low and soft.

Gep's eyes lock onto mine and I try to keep the guilt from my face. Christ! Is this from what I said? It can't be and yet, it feels like a huge co-incidence. Too huge.

'Shut the back door. Now. Stay quiet.'

The knock comes again, but we stay where we are, shutting the door with a soft click. And wait. One more knock, like three's the charm, and then we hear footsteps walking away and a car starting.

Gep stares at me and I'm the first to look away, proving my guilt to him. 'This isn't over, Penn. But I'll deal with you later.' He claps his hands, one exclamation point to his anger. 'One hour to pack whatever shit you can and then we're out of here.'

And I know our life isn't going to change. As much as I want it to, we're moving on to the next town in the dark of night like we always do; the bad guys making their getaway, leaving grief and anger in our wake, with spirits and the burn and Gep controlling our future. And I'll stay because it's the only way I can keep Jimmy safe.

Something's got to change. Has too! I just don't know what that something will be.

'Blue'—Penn's story—is available in both e-book and paperback.

What would you do to protect your family?

17-year-old Penn just wants a real life. One where he's not forced to lie and steal for his abusive stepfather, Gep. One where he and his twin brother, Jimmy, are free from Gep's dark magic.

When they move to yet another town to steal magical artefacts for Gep, Penn is hopeful that things might be different this time. Especially when he finds himself attracted to a girl in his class, Selti.

But when Jimmy starts to weaken, fading like their mum did before she died, Penn knows he'll do anything to save him. Even if that means betraying Selti...or giving in to his own powers.

A modern retelling of Pinocchio with an urban fantasy twist.

Forever Flying

Nick

My hands shake like I've had six double shots of coffee and I jam them in my pockets so that Grace, when she gets here, won't notice. With my heart feeling like it's trying to pound its way out of my chest, I can't stop pacing along the top of the cliff, back and forth, back and forth, as if this is somehow going to make me feel better. At this rate, I'm going to have walked a definite path in the grass by the time she gets here. I don't know why I'm so nervous. Stupid really.

We've been together three years and after all the shit thay happened at the beginning of our relationship, we're good. More than good. She's mine and I'm hers. I know she's going to say yes. Know it! And yet...

I wonder, for half a second, whether I've got time to go flying. Just shed all my clothes and take off. Revelling in the other side of me would definitely calm my nerves. Except, knowing my luck, I'd get the timing wrong and have to propose naked. Not that that's really a problem but it doesn't quite have the same romantic feel I'm going for.

I shake my head. Three years ago, the thought of doing something romantic like this would've had me rolling my eyes and yet, for Grace...for Grace I want to do this and more. I need her to know how much she means to me. How much I love her.

I look at my watch. Fifteen minutes to go. God, why'd I get here so frigging early?

I spin around at the sound of a car but it's only Dad. I lean over, hands on my knees for a moment, trying to get my heart to understand that everything's okay.

Dad chuckles as he gets out of the car. Arse.

'Bit nervous there?'

I stand back up and glare at him. 'Shut up.'

He just laughs again and wraps me in a hug. 'I remember being shit scared when I proposed to your mum.'

'Really?'

'Yep. Didn't think I was going to actually be able to talk, my mouth was so dry.'

'Yeah. But *you* knew Mum was going to say yes. The bond was for both of you.'

He clasps my shoulders in both hands and looks at me. 'She's going to say yes, Nick. You don't go through all you've both gone through without loving each other.'

I nod; more of a jerk of my head actually, but he gets the idea. He nods back and taps my shoulders before dropping his hands.

'It looks great. She's going to love it.'

I take a deep breath. He's right. She is going to.

I hope so anyway.

Grace

My grandmother sits with her hands clasped in her lap and a small smile on her face in the passenger seat.

'You truly aren't going to tell me what Nick's got planned for my birthday?'

She looks over at me and then turns back to the front, Mona-Lisa smile firmly in place.

I groan. 'Lily! Come on. You know I hate surprises.'

'You'll love this one.'

The knot in my stomach tightens and I press my lips together. What if I don't? If I knew what it was, I could prepare, think about how I needed to react. Why the hell has Nick set up a surprise for my birthday? Of all the ridiculous, crazy things...

I sigh. I'm being stupid. I have a fantastic, loving boyfriend who does romantic things for me and I'm bitching about not knowing what's planned.

'Get it together, Grace,' I mutter under my breath.

Lily turns to me. 'Did you say something, gorgeous girl?'

I shake my head and flick on the radio. If Lily isn't going to talk, I need some noise to fill the empty space that's allowing me far too much thinking time.

I drive up the last part of the hill to the cliff which I've come to think of as ours, despite the fact that we share it with all of Bruny Island. This is the place where Nick saved my life, where we'd been flying so many times, where he'd taken those beautiful photos of me playing my violin.

We crest the hill, the ocean stretching out in front of us, and I see Nick. And even though we'd been together that afternoon, the sight of him dressed in jeans and a white button-up shirt with the sleeves rolled up, his dark hair blowing in the breeze, is enough to make everything in me tighten for a totally different reason.

Even after three years.

I get out of the car and hear Lily get out as well. The grassed area has different things set up around it and standing a few metres behind Nick is Henry. I frown and wave at Henry. He waves back, a smile on his face.

Nick

Now she's here, my nerves fall away as if they've never existed. Just the sight of her, frowning as she takes everything in and tries to make sense of it, is so familiar that it takes everything in me not to just walk forward and wrap her in my arms.

I smile at her and she smiles back, a trace of the frown still there.

'Hey.'

'Happy birthday.' I reach out to touch her cheek as she gets closer, and she leans into my touch.

'You've already said that to me today. Probably twenty times already.' She puts her hand over mine and I clasp her fingers and bring them to my lips.

'Twenty-one times for good luck, then.'

She laughs, like I knew she would.

'So, what's all this?'

I look at Lily and she nods, knowing what she needs to do. She'd been so excited when I'd asked her to be a part of this. But she's such an important person in Grace's life that there's no way I'd do it without her.

She unties the end of the ribbon from the garden stake beside me and passes it to Grace, who takes it, rubbing the satin between her fingers. The frown's back on her face and I chuckle, gently smoothing it away with my fingers.

'Just go with it, okay? You'll like it. I promise.'

She screws her nose up at me and then smiles. 'Okay, okay.'

Lily touches her arm. 'My gorgeous girl, I have loved every minute I've had you with me. I'm so proud of you and of the beautiful young woman you are. Happy twenty-first birthday. I love you.'

I can see the tears in Grace's eyes as she leans down to give Lily a hug.

'Love you too.'

Lily squeezes her hand as they separate. 'Enjoy your night.'

Grace

She walks over to Henry's car and sits in the passenger seat. I frown again and look back at Nick. He's grinning at me, and I slap his arm gently, the frown sliding away.

'I know, I know. But what's going on?'

He winks at me. 'You'll see.'

That's obviously Henry's cue because he walks over to us, his smile as wide as Nick's.

'Hey, Grace.'

'Hey, Henry. I'm assuming you know what's going on here?'

He chuckles. 'Yep.'

'And you're not going to tell me either?'

'Nope.' His grin gets wider if that's possible and he hugs me before taking my hand, holding the ribbon between us. 'I can say though, that despite me being an idiot when you first came into Nick's life, I'm glad you're part of our family. I couldn't ask for someone better to love Nick. Happy birthday.'

He hands me a small box. I hug him in thanks and open it. Inside, a silver bracelet with a small violin charm sparkles in the late afternoon sun

'It's beautiful.'

He smiles. 'I'm glad you like it. Now, we're going to leave you young people to enjoy your night.'

He kisses me on the cheek and joins Lily in the car. We watch in silence as they drive off and then Nick reaches for my hand, rubbing his thumb across the top in a way that makes me feel loved.

'Are you ready?'

I laugh. 'I don't know. Am I?'

He grins and gestures to the area he's set up.

'All you have to do is follow the ribbon and see what you find.'

A shiver of excitement passes over me and I grin back at him. 'That sounds easy enough.'

With Nick at my side, I start walking.

Nick

She comes to the first table and lets out a soft breath at the feather encased in resin that I had made into a necklace for her. It's one of mine, of course, and she picks it up, running her finger over it.

'There's a date engraved on the back,' I say and she turns it over. 'It's the day I first shared what I am with you. Something I've never regretted. I love that you know that side of me.'

She turns and I secure it around her neck.

'I love it.' She kisses me. A long one that has me thinking about just rushing through to the end of the tour and getting back home with her. I pull back and let out a shuddering laugh, the longing in it evident, even to myself. Jesus, even after three years, I've still got it bad for her.

'If you keep doing that, we'll never get to the end.'

She laughs with me and doesn't look at all remorseful. But she does follow the ribbon again. We're kissing again at the next stop – a serving of the first dessert we'd shared and the one we still share when we go out; sticky date pudding.

We eat it together under the light of the setting sun, mixed in with kisses and laughing and it's as good as I'd hoped it'd be.

And then we continue; listening to the recording I'd made of her first violin solo after she'd been accepted at the Conservatorium of Music at Tassie Uni; unwrapping a bottle of her favourite perfume – the one that always reminds me of Grace; a photo stand, where I've set up stupid accessories so we can take funny photos of us together. She laughs so much during this that I can't stop smiling myself, my heart already feeling like it's flying sky high even if the rest of me is still on the ground.

And then we're at the end of the ribboned course and Grace looks around, a small frown back on her face.

I take a deep breath. This is it.

Grace

My cheeks hurt with all the smiling and laughing I've done. I can't believe he's organised all of this for me. This special man who, with some obviously well-thought-out pushes from fate, has become one of the most important people in my life. I turn to him as we come to the end of the ribbon and he clears his throat, dragging his fingers through his hair in a way that I know means he's nervous. I put my hand on his chest and can feel his heart pounding.

'Grace,' he starts and the way he says it, raspy and low, like he's barely controlling his love for me, means that I move closer, unable to help myself, hand slipping under his shirt so that I can run my fingers over the muscles at the top of his jeans, my lips finding his again. He groans, returning the kiss for moments before pushing me gently away.

'Jesus, Grace, you're making this hard.'

I raise my eyebrows at him. 'Am I?'

He chokes out a laugh and shakes his head.

'I have to give you your final present.'

'You could be my final present.'

He grins. 'Okay, maybe second last present then.'

It's my turn to laugh and I take half a step back. 'I'm keeping you to that.'

Then, as if we're part of a romantic movie, the sun finally sets and he touches something in his pocket. Fairy lights come on around us, surrounding us with twinkles of light, in our own little world. I smile at him but it falls away as he sinks to one knee in front of me, my breath catching in my throat.

And then, he's bringing a case out of his pocket and when he opens it, it holds a ring so perfect for me that I have no doubt he knows me better than anyone. Knows who I am. It's a rose gold band with a single diamond, sparkling in the lights. Simple. Elegant.

'Grace, there isn't a day since we met when I'm not grateful that you came into my life. I love you and it'd make me so incredibly proud if you'd call me your husband. Come flying with me forever, Grace?'

I kneel down with him and take his face in my hands, touching his lips gently with mine. I don't have to think about my answer for a second.

'Yes.'

And when he kisses me, I decide I might like surprises after all.

See where it all began with Grace and Nick's story - Aquila

Acknowledgments

Even though being an author is essentially, a solitary activity (after all, no one else can hear your characters whispering their stories), this is not something I'd ever be able to do without being surrounded by some absolutely fantastic human beings.

My family - Adrian, Jack, Gabrielle and Lawson, all of whom support me in so many beautiful ways - how did I get so lucky? Mum and Dad, who have never doubted (or at least, never let on if they have!). And to the rest of my family - like a beautiful, huge web of love - for everything that you do, little and big, it is so appreciated.

My friends - what would I do without you guys? For your support, your feedback, your enthusiasm, your love, your laughter and for supplying a good cup of tea or glass of wine at times when it's most needed, know that I won't be able to ever offer enough appreciation (but I'll keep trying!)

My readers - without you, I'd just be someone who hears stories in their head! Thank you to my returning readers and to my new readers - I hope you enjoyed reading these stores as much as I enjoyed writing them. Big (massive, huge!) love and thanks to you all.

About the Author

A writer of copious amounts of words – just because if they didn't come out, she's sure they'd make her head explode – Sue-Ellen is an internationally published author.

In her 'other' life, she is a social worker living in Central Queensland with her family, two dogs and a snake called Slide.

She loves quirky shoes, dark chocolate and good tea. An eternal optimist, she enjoys making things difficult for her protagonists but loves a satisfying ending.

You can find Sue-Ellen at:

www.sueellenpashley.com.au
https://www.facebook.com/sueellenpashleyauthor
Instagram – sueellenpashleyauthor

Also by Sue-Ellen Pashley

www.ingramcontent.com/pod-product-compliance
Lightning Source LLC
Chambersburg PA
CBHW070032120726
47909CB00003B/1132